"YOU MAY NOT WANT ME NOW, BUT, BY GOD, YOU'RE GOING TO WANT ME. I'M GOING TO MAKE YOU WANT ME!"

His hands slid down her bare arms to the curve of her hips. Then, slowly, tantalizingly, they started teasing upward along her spine, all the while pressing her closer into his hard muscles. His lips smothered hers, stealing the breath and the words from her in one swift demand. Searle's mouth parted in ardent response and she trembled.

"No more protests, Searle, no more denials," Buck rasped softly. "This time you'll melt for me. . . ."

A STRANGE ELATION

Prudence Martin

A CANDLELIGHT ECSTASY ROMANCE™

Published by
Dell Publishing Co., Inc.
1 Dag Hammarskjold Plaza
New York, New York 10017

ISBN: 0-440-17505-4

Printed in the United States of America
First printing—November 1982

To Our Readers:

We have been delighted with your enthusiastic response to Candlelight Ecstasy Romances™, and we thank you for the interest you have shown in this exciting series.

In the upcoming months we will continue to present the distinctive sensuous love stories you have come to expect only from Ecstasy. We look forward to bringing you many more books from your favorite authors and also the very finest work from new authors of contemporary romantic fiction.

As always, we are striving to present the unique, absorbing love stories that you enjoy most—books that are more than ordinary romance.

Your suggestions and comments are always welcome. Please write to us at the address below.

Sincerely,

The Editors
Candlelight Romances
1 Dag Hammarskjold Plaza
New York, New York 10017

CHAPTER ONE

Heels clicked against linoleum with an efficient staccato that told them she was coming. Heads swiveled, eyes fixed on the glass door at the end of the long, desk-filled room. Their patience was soon rewarded. Searle Delacorte swept in like a sultry south wind.

Male eyes filled with appreciation as she passed by, stretching out her long legs in a stride that in any other woman would have been thought aggressive. Like everything else about her, Searle's stride was seductive. Even her practical cotton tunic and skirt exuded a sex appeal that elicited sighs of envy from the females in the crowded room. The black of her top and skirt seemed to reflect back into the deep blue-black of her hair. As always when at work, Searle had twisted her thick mass of hair into a slick roll; every man she walked past knew a moment of longing to kiss the slender neck thus exposed. Every one of them knew it was an impossible dream.

"Snow Queen" was what they called her behind her back. Searle rarely dated a man more than once, and those she had, reported receiving nothing more than a dutiful dusting of her overfull red lips. It was not that Searle would not have liked more. She avoided getting involved simply because she had long ago decided that sex was highly overrated. It usually led to complications she would rather do without.

She paused before a door with gold letters boldly proclaiming EDITOR. With one imperative rap, Searle entered before the expected response of "come in" could be heard. A collective sigh whistled through the room as the door snapped shut behind her.

The gray head bent over the cluttered desk didn't look

up. The pen rolling across the page didn't pause in its movement. Searle's eyes narrowed. Lenn Roberts only rarely employed this tactic of making her wait to be noticed—usually when he had something to say that he knew she wouldn't want to hear, she thought with a sinking feeling. She crossed to slip fluidly into the nearest chair, hoping he wasn't going to ask her to do another feature on the singles scene.

Her worry did not transmit itself to her exquisite features. Roberts saw only the usual composed intelligence when he at last set aside his pen and raised his head. Even then he did not speak but leaned back into the soft leather of his chair and studied the young woman before him. Not for the first time, he wondered why she was so lovely. She shouldn't be, he reasoned, taking each of her features by itself. Every item was slightly off-balance, as if placed haphazardly into her face. Beneath arched brows, her wide emerald eyes slanted up at each end, rather like those of a watchful cat's. Prominent bones marred the svelte plains of her cheeks. The long, straight nose sat off-center above the closed lips, while the full bottom lip definitely overshadowed the narrower top one. Yet they all came together to a stunning effect. He noticed the heavy lids dropping over the cat's eyes and knew Searle was becoming impatient. With a broad smile, he sat forward.

"I looked over that piece you did on changing architecture in the city parks," he commented.

Searle's full lower lip thrust out, then slid upward in a languorous smile. "Oh?" she responded in a husky contralto.

"It was damn good," Lenn said briefly.

"I know," she said calmly.

The gray head tilted with laughter. Crinkles of enjoyment embedded themselves beside the lines marking either side of his wide mouth. Prisms of light glinted across the gold-rimmed glasses to highlight his pale blue eyes. Searle waited patiently for him to calm down, saying nothing.

"Ah, Searle, if I only had a whole staff like you! Usually, I'm having to bolster the writer's sagging confidence . . ." His voice dropped away to chuckle once more. Then he settled back into the depths of his chair, ran a hand over the thinning gray-white hair, and suddenly looked serious. "I need you to handle the feature interview for the September issue."

"Terrific." Searle was sitting upright now, attentive. "Who is it?"

Robert's eyes slid away from her, unable to meet the intense, aggressive green gaze.

"Bucky Carlton."

A puzzled line traced across her brow. "Who?"

"Buck Carlton, the Blues' right fielder."

"The Blues?" she repeated, feeling like a student who'd forgotten to prepare for the exam. Bewilderment slowly gave way to understanding. "The baseball team? A baseball player? You want *me* to interview a baseball player?" she finished in disbelief.

"Well, Searle, he's—"

"No way, Lenn, uh-uh," cut in Searle with a decisive shake of her head. "I'm not—repeat, not—a sportswriter."

"You are, however, the best writer *Our Town*'s got and I'm handing this assignment to you," said Roberts firmly.

"Why me? Why not Garrison?"

"He broke his leg doing that backpacking piece. I need someone *now.*"

"Then use Jim Wheeler or Doug Evers from the paper staff or—"

"Or you."

"But I know *nothing* about baseball! Which is precisely the way I'd like to keep it." She saw no hint of understanding on the older man's lined face. He must have, she decided, suffered sunstroke or something. Asking *her* to interview some jock! The outraged shock shone clearly in the slanting angry eyes. She turned her gaze to the plate-glass window, scarcely noticing the distant city skyline rising beyond the green slopes.

The editor stared at his writer, amusement coloring his eyes. He had rarely seen Searle Delacorte discomposed and he was fully enjoying the novelty. Long, tapering fingers drummed impatiently on her kneecap while her rigid body language fairly shouted her indignation.

"This isn't to be a story about the game, Searle," he said in a coaxing tone, "but a feature on the man. That sort of in-depth character study is your strong point. It shouldn't matter what this fellow does so much as who he is."

Her eyes remained fixed on the window just long enough to let him know she wasn't to be flattered. Then she faced him with apparent disinterest. "So what's so special about this Carlton that we're doing a feature on him?"

"What's so special—? You must be joking!" exclaimed Lenn, staring at her in amazement.

"I don't read the sports page," she said defensively.

"Carlton's been *front* page news the last few weeks. He's on the hottest hitting streak since Ted Williams in the forties."

"Great," she said flatly. Searle examined the shine of her black patent leather heels, then suggested in her low, musical voice, "How about giving this to a free-lancer who happens to like baseball?"

"Searle, I want you to do this. Carlton doesn't grant too many interviews—frankly, I was surprised when he agreed to let *Our Town* see him. I haven't got time to waste hunting up another capable writer. He may change his mind and I'm not taking that chance." Lenn straightened, palmed his pen and a bundle of paper in one practiced motion. "Be at the stadium this afternoon at five. It's arranged for him to meet you before tonight's game."

She took a deep breath and rose. "You want the personal side?" she inquired icily.

Roberts answered without looking up. "Bucky Carlton's rich, successful, and single. A man at the top. I want you to bring out the personal side of the professional athlete."

The pen began crossing a page, signaling the end of the discussion. With a frustrated sigh, Searle strode out, again bringing a brief silence to the room beyond the editor's door. The eyes of those along her route focused on the alluring curves of her receding form. For once, she truly wasn't aware of her effect. Searle was far too busy trying to convince herself that she would do a good job on the unwanted piece.

I love my job, I love my job, she wryly told herself as she entered her closetlike office. In truth, Searle did love her job. In her two years at Midwest Publishing, she had risen rapidly, achieving more than any other female writer hired there. She had started as a society/general story reporter for a number of the company's eleven suburban weekly newspapers. It had not been long before Lenn Roberts had requested her transfer to work for him on the company's premier publication, the monthly *Our Town* magazine. With a little bargaining on her part, she'd been given her private square of working space along with her advance in status.

Her eyes moved from the long, tall file cabinet, crowned with Swedish ivy, to the organized clutter of her desk, to the dust cover on her typewriter. Though many of the reporters now typed directly into a computerized keyboard, Searle preferred the crisp, exciting feel of a typed page freshly yanked from her IBM Selectric. She felt she could make a more critical judgment staring at the typed sheet rather than at the oddly green block letters on a video screen. That seemed too cold, too lifeless for her. A thought that would have shocked her fellow employees, most of whom were certain Searle Delacorte was as mechanical as any videosetter.

Midwest Publishing was a large organization, what was known in the business as a "complete shop." In addition to the editorial staffs for newspapers and magazine, the company employed people for advertising, bookkeeping, circulation, composition, camera, and presses, all housed in three buildings on the northern edge of town. But of the more than two hundred employees, Searle had remained aloof and alone. No buddies, no confidantes, and certainly no lovers.

As if on cue, her thoughts were disrupted by a ready knock. Since her door was usually approached hesitantly, she knew it had to be Norman Kraekor. The middle-aged ad executive never seemed to give up, she thought as she bid him to come in.

"Well, well, honey, have you thought about the tickets I've got for the Philharmonic tonight?" His polished grin of invitation split across his swarthy features. Ten in the morning and already his thin cheeks were covered with five o'clock shadow, she noted with mild distaste.

With a sudden feeling of gratitude toward her imperious editor, Searle shook her head as she took her seat behind her desk. "I'm sorry, Norm. Lenn's set up an interview with some ballplayer. I figure I'll have to stay for the game and that shoots the night for me." She had no such intention, but a little lie was better than an evening spent dodging Norman's clumsy advances.

The grin dissolved. "Ah, honey, that's too bad. I was counting on you." The gold chains swung about his neck as he sat opposite her on the room's one plastic chair. He rapidly searched through a mental list of women he could possibly take to a symphony concert. Halfway through, he gave it up, eyeing Searle with speculation in his pale gray eyes. "Hey, babe, how's about I come with you? Sort of keep you from gettin' bored. I could even give you a few pointers on the ol' ball game."

Sunlight from the window behind her splayed across her desk and over Norman, emphasizing the wrinkles creasing his face and unfairly revealing the lighter roots beneath the black dye of his thick hair. He looked like some overeager schoolboy, and with an almost pitying thankfulness, Searle again shook her head.

"When I'm on a story, I can't have any distractions. I need to explore the game in my own way, Norm." She felt a stab of guilt as she saw his crestfallen expression. He was, after all, a nice guy beneath the playboy flash. Hadn't he gotten those Philharmonic tickets just for her? With a smile she added, "Maybe some other time."

"So what's this story you're doing?" he asked, wondering how he could pin her down for another date. Since their one date several months ago, he hadn't given up hope of convincing her to go out again. Just the memory of her as she had looked that night, in a long, clingy gown, with her midnight hair waving over her shoulders, made his throat go dry.

"Oh, an interview with some jock named Duke—no, Buck. Buck Carlton."

"Carlton? You're interviewing the town's most eligible bachelor?" His voice held his displeasure at the thought.

"Oh, is he?" said Searle mechanically. "I really can't say I know anything about the man." She removed the cover from her IBM, smiling coolly at Norman as she neatly folded it. He ignored the hint.

"All the more reason you need a few tips from me, honey," he said, thinking quickly. "How's about I fill you in on the celebrated Carlton over lunch?" His confidence was returning; one of the few things widely known about Searle Delacorte was her highbrow taste. She preferred champagne to beer, ballet to disco, and, clearly, almost anything to sports. His fear of competition from the major-leaguer evaporated. To her, Bucky Carlton was merely "some jock," a distasteful assignment. Displaying his capped teeth in a glorious grin, Kraekor prodded, "I could pick you up at noon."

Searle inwardly sighed, weighing the options. To go would doubtlessly encourage him, a thing she most definitely did not want to do. On the other hand, to go would mean she could use the morning to put the finishing touches on her "Dining Out in the City" column rather than reading old news clippings on the player. It might also provide an excuse to keep Norman out of her hair for another couple of months. That thought clinched it.

"All right, Norm, I'd appreciate your help. And now," she added firmly, "I have to get to work or I won't have any time for lunch."

"Okay, baby! I'll see you at noon." With his toothy smile and a whistle, he disappeared.

Searle turned to her typewriter and promptly forgot everything but trying to recapture the pleasures of eating at the elegant Grand Restaurant. She was reading over the last page, feeling pleased with the result, when Norman's brisk tattoo again sounded.

"Hey, babes, you ready?" he asked as he stuck his head around her door.

"Certainly." She paper-clipped her typed pages together, set them on the corner of her desk, and covered her machine. Norman appreciated the fluidity of each movement Searle made and found himself again wondering if she retained that cool grace in bed. He didn't really believe he'd ever have the chance to find out, but there were always miracles.

They walked together to his sporty car without touching. Searle didn't invite such intimacies and Norm knew better than to press. They talked shop during the short drive to a nearby Mexican restaurant, a favorite noontime eatery of the company's employees. They nodded to a number of co-workers as they were led to their booth, Kraekor unable to resist grinning victoriously at his male cohorts.

Once they were seated alone, with the business of selecting and ordering out of the way and two large margaritas standing before them, Searle didn't waste further time. "Tell me about this Bucky Carlton," she commanded.

"Well, he's one of the Blues' best players," replied Norm, sipping his well-iced drink. "Been with the team for about five years and always been consistently good. This year he just happens to be consistently great."

"You said he was the town's most eligible bachelor," she prompted.

"Yeah, well, the guy's been no dummy. He's invested his earnings wisely and during the off-season he makes endorsements and commercials for local companies. Now he's doing national ads, too. So, you have a man who's still relatively young—"

"How young?"

"Thirtyish, give or take a year. And he's wealthy. And he's very well-liked in the community."

"Why is that?"

Norm played with his straw in his drink. To Searle it seemed a strangely feminine action, at odds with his carefully cultivated macho image. "He does benefits, charity appearances, all that stuff. Plus he moved here."

The waitress appeared and Searle waited for her to put down their heaping dishes and leave before asking, "Don't all the ballplayers live here?"

"Nah, not usually. A player just works for a team, honey, and with trades and short careers and all, he doesn't usually put down roots in a team town. A number of the Blues do have homes locally, though, and Carlton scored a big one with the fans when he built one here a few years ago."

The subdued lighting darkened Searle's hair and heightened his desire for her. To thaw out the Snow Queen, that would be a feat! He watched her lips press against her glass—she always shunned using a straw—and he downed the end of his drink at a gulp. "You want another margarita, honey?"

"No, thanks. What does this paragon of a player do for pleasure?"

Norman laughed, a leering kind of laugh that brought the lids sliding down over Searle's slanted eyes. *What on earth,* she wondered.

"Ah, babes, off-field Carlton's got one game—women. He's a love 'em-and-leave 'em playboy, so it's kind of hard to keep track, but so far this season he's been through a New York model and a Las Vegas showgirl. Or so the stories go." He noted with satisfaction the distaste that was evident on Searle's expressive face. He decided to press the point. "A few years ago one of his less-pleased castoffs took him to court with a paternity suit, but it was quickly and quietly settled. Surprisingly, the press dropped the incident. I don't even know if he acknowledged the kid or not."

The rest of the meal passed uneventfully, Searle digesting the information Kraekor had so glibly divulged and Norman trying unsuccessfully to get a date with her for the weekend. He gave up only as he deposited her back in her tiny office, accepting with a shrug her final "I'll probably be wrapped up in getting this interview to Lenn."

She put Norman and his revelations out of her mind for the afternoon, concentrating on her work. When the rapid click of her IBM sounded, nothing and no one dared intrude. Her ability to devote herself to a single story to the exclusion of all else had placed her in the position of being the first woman promoted to her level at Midwest Publishing. It was her one pride.

But Searle returned to the subject of Bucky Carlton as

she drove in her white Toyota to Blues' Stadium as directed later that day. *What grown man would have a name like Bucky?* she scornfully thought. Driving through the ball park gates, she easily pictured the kind of man he would be—a big, beefy all-male athlete who no doubt spoke a murdered English. She just hoped he didn't chew tobacco. But he probably did, she thought with another sigh as she parked, then walked to the press entrance.

She showed her pass to the security man there, then waited impatiently while he placed a confirming call. The concrete, bowl-shaped structure offended her, but she tried to erase her prejudice from her mind. As Lenn said, it shouldn't matter if this guy was a ballplayer. But somehow it did and, irritated, Searle once more wondered how Lenn could have been so insane.

Dropping the phone into its cradle, the guard asked her to follow him. Wordlessly, he led her down a narrow passageway, the echoing of her heels against the concrete providing an eerie rhythm. Rounding a corner, the guard paused.

"There's Mr. Carlton now, miss."

CHAPTER TWO

He was exactly what she had expected. Shoulders stretched from East Coast to West. Biceps bulged beneath the rolled-up shirt sleeves. Sun-bleached golden hair waved about the tanned square face and tossed casually over his broad brow. There was even, she thought with a shade of morose satisfaction, the expected boyish grin planted below the thick sandy moustache. All brawn and no brain, she summed up as her eyes, having surveyed him from head to toe, now traveled disdainfully back up to meet his.

In startling contrast to the blond hair, dark brown eyes smiled down at her. Behind the smile, his eyes glittered with a look Searle knew well. His first words as he came toward her confirmed the look.

"This is going to be one interview I'm going to enjoy." He reminded her of the big bad wolf smacking his lips hungrily at Little Red Riding Hood. Slowly, his gaze crept over her, assessing each inch with an experienced calculation. As his eyes came back to hers, Searle realized hotly that she'd just been undressed by a professional.

With a mental resolve to wring Lenn Roberts's neck in the morning, Searle extended her hand. "Mr. Carlton, I'm Searle Delacorte from *Our Town* magazine."

Her hand was enclosed in a massive grip. Inexplicably, she shivered and tried to snatch her hand free. Carlton held on more firmly, foiling her attempts to reclaim her hand. He stared down at her, a dangerous dark glint in the brown eyes. When he spoke, the words came from deep in his throat.

"Your voice is sweeter and thicker than a jar of honey."

A mixture of unexplainable emotions surged through

her, but anger emerged uppermost. His look, his words insulted her professionalism, and Searle pulled her hand from his grasp wrathfully. She opened her mouth, about to tell him the interview was off, when a commotion erupted with the appearance of a noisy trio of men. The three stopped a few feet away, eyeing Searle and Carlton in open curiosity. Throwing them a crooked smile over his shoulder, Carlton took possession of Searle's arm.

"I think we'd better move somewhere more private for our interview, Miss Delacorte," he said as he took a step away from the direction of the three.

"Hey-ee, Bucky ol' man," called out a voice from the trio, "how'd you rate a dish like that?"

"By doing something you seem to have given up, Johnson—connecting with my bat," answered Buck. He flashed a broad, triumphant male grin that made Searle long to slap him.

"And just which *bat* is that?" demanded the other.

Amid the jeering laughs and howls, Searle Delacorte, who had forgotten how to blush before she was sixteen, felt the telltale heat mount her cheeks. She raised her head high and condemned them all with a gelid glare. If she must be subjected to such sophomoric jokes—and what else could be expected from men who played childish games for a living?—then at least she would not give them the satisfaction of seeing her flustered. Or so she hoped.

Carlton was still chuckling as he steered her around a corner and through a door marked PRIVATE. Inside, a round table and a few straight chairs provided the decor. A counter ran along one wall and a stained coffeemaker stood forlornly atop it. Her anger subsided as Searle took in the businesslike surroundings. Taking the chair Carlton held out for her, she reached into her handbag and withdrew a notebook and pen. With an efficient snap, she opened the book and held her pen poised.

"I'd like to confirm a few facts, Mr. Carlton, before

proceeding to the questions I've prepared. You've played for the Blues for five seasons?" she asked. He nodded, fixing his gaze on her with a disconcerting intensity. "You have, in that time, established yourself as a mainstay of the team, a regular player? You—"

"These are things you could find out on the back of any bubble-gum card," he broke in abruptly. "Haven't you done your homework, Miss Delacorte?"

Clenching her notebook tightly, Searle refrained from hitting him with it as she realized with a guilty start that he was right. This was the only interview she'd ever gone into without thoroughly checking her subject's background. That he was right only infuriated her more and she met his amused gaze with her haughtiest look.

"Have you always wanted to play baseball?" she asked coldly.

"Sure. Why not? It's fun, I play well, and I make a helluva lot more money than sitting at some desk nine to five all day." He rested his square chin on the palm of his hand and watched her jot his quote in her book. "How about you? You always wanted to be a reporter?"

"We are here, Mr. Carlton, to interview *you,*" she reminded him in icy tones. Looking up from her abbreviated scribblings, Searle was annoyed to find him steadily staring at her, looking more pleased than the Cheshire cat. "About the personal side of Buck Carlton," she said in a voice designed to get his mind back to business, "how do you spend your free time after a game?"

"Come with me tonight and I'll personally show you," he replied. The gleam in his eyes spoke volumes, all of them X-rated.

"No thank you, Mr.—"

"Buck."

"Mr. Carlton," she said firmly. "I'll do quite well enough if you'll just answer the questions."

"I'm sure, Miss Delacorte, you could do much better

with me showing you," he said in a low, stroking voice. He paused as anger sparked the green eyes frowning at him. "Usually, I just go home, watch a little TV, maybe read a little, then hit the hay."

Swallowing her desire to express surprise that he could read, she raised a disbelieving brow. "That sounds awfully tame for a man of your reputation."

"So you have done your homework," he remarked approvingly. "You married?" he added in an offhand manner.

"That, Mr. Carlton, is none of your business," Searle answered through clenched teeth.

"I didn't think so," Buck commented with a satisfied nod. "You've probably chased off every man who's come within six feet of you."

"About your evenings!" snapped Searle.

"Oh, once in a while I've stopped at a club or two, been seen with a beautiful woman and so established myself as a party-going playboy." Buck shrugged, then chuckled. "I was pretty wild a few years ago and the press hasn't forgotten it. Today I'm basically very dull. But that's not to say I don't enjoy going out and having a good time," he added with a suggestive smile.

"When you do want to have a 'good time,' what do you do? Where do you go?"

"Have you got a steady guy?" he asked in return.

She tried to control the trembling in her hands. If Lenn thought she would put up with such insolent, arrogant—

"Forget him," commanded Buck Carlton, cutting through her hostile thoughts. "Come out with me tonight, Searle."

"The name, Mr. Carlton, is Miss Delacorte," she clipped in a voice as friendly as a Mideast conflict.

"Sure, Searle. Look, I've gotta go get changed for the game," he said, standing.

"But the interview!" she protested.

"We'll work on it after the game."

"But I'm not—"

He strode to the door, then turned and grinned. "I'll hit a homer for you, Searle," he promised.

"But—"

He was gone. She sat seething, striving to regain her composure. She shut her notebook with an angry crack. She'd never before lost control of an interview and the sensation was distinctly unpleasant. That some towering, oversized jock should treat her like a common pickup was too much. She'd tell Lenn to take Buck Carlton and—

The click of the door behind her startled her. Whirling, she experienced faint disappointment to see a teenage boy in an usher's uniform standing there.

"Miss Delacorte? If you'd like to watch the warm-ups, I'll escort you to your seat."

"But I haven't purchased a ticket yet."

"That's been taken care of. Mr. Carlton arranged for you to sit in the best first-baseline box seat." The boy was obviously impressed.

Rapidly, Searle considered the situation. If she did go out with the big ape tonight, she could have this story wrapped up and on Lenn's desk by Friday. Refusing to acknowledge any other reason for the sudden tingle of anticipation she felt, Searle rose and presented the usher with her prettiest smile.

Soon, she was sitting front row in a field box seat, reading through a program that the teenager had thoughtfully given her. From it, she learned that Buck Carlton, six-foot-one and one hundred eighty-five pounds, hailed from Grants Pass, Oregon. In the brief statistical bio she discovered that he had been selected for the All-Star team the last four years in a row and that he was styled an aggressive, all-out player. This she could believe. In her brief encounter with Buck Carlton, Searle had already learned he was the type of man to get what he wanted, to take it if he had to. The memory of him staring at her, desirously stripping her with his dark eyes, sent another tremor through her. Really, she scolded with a touch of nervousness, anyone would think she was an adolescent on prom night the way she was acting!

Putting the vision of Carlton's searing eyes out of her mind, Searle focused on the stadium. It was a modern facility with computerized scoreboard, artificial turf, and bright lights running over the Blues' emblem on the high wall surrounding the outfield. Players of both teams were on the field, some taking turns in the batting cage, others sprinting and throwing balls in the outfield. This was going to be one long, boring night, she thought with a sigh. Looking around, she saw fans beginning to trickle in, especially over in the general admission seats. Her eye caught sight of a man with a hot dog and a Coke, and Searle realized with a pang that she hadn't eaten since lunch. Leaving her program on her seat, she moved to the concession stands back inside the concourse.

As she disappeared from view, Buck Carlton came out of the Blues' dugout. His eyes went immediately to the empty field box seat. With an oath, he swung himself over the wall and stalked to the chair. He stared down at the program, then as his angry eyes came up, he saw the usher he'd sent in to Searle.

"You, kid!" he called imperatively.

The young boy scrambled down the concrete steps and over to the player. "Yes, sir?"

"Where is Miss Delacorte? Didn't you get her as I asked?"

"Y-yes, sir," stammered the usher. He watched the muscles twitching in Carlton's cheek and added rapidly, "I-I brought her here, sir. That's the program I gave her."

"Well, dammit, where is she?" demanded Buck, as much of himself as of the boy.

"Carlton, are you playing or watching tonight's game?" asked a dry voice.

Looking down to find his manager calmly eyeing him, Buck shrugged, then leaped lithely back down to the field. Joey Howe stared in amazement at the back of his star hitter as Buck strode to the batting cage. Carlton's even temperament made him well-liked with the coaching staff as well as with teammates, and his evident anger surprised the manager. He turned to ask the usher what was up, but the boy had vanished.

By the time Searle returned to her seat, the players were off the field and people were filing into the stadium in earnest. She had eaten in the concourse, washed up in the surprisingly clean ladies' room, and now carried only her purse and a soda. Ground crews were finishing their preparations on the diamond and a swell of excited expectation rose over the stadium.

A group of men claimed the seats next to hers in the box. All of them eyed her with the speculation she had grown used to seeing in men's eyes, but miraculously none made any attempt to make a pass. Since her box was just to the right of the Blues' dugout, Buck couldn't see Searle until the players were announced for the game. As he came out onto the field, his steely gaze riveted on that first-baseline box seat. Seeing her sitting there, her hands folded calmly atop her program, a broad grin lifted the ends of his sandy moustache and the steel went out of his eyes. For a moment, Searle wished she hadn't stayed for the game.

The wishful moment became a full-blown desire as, after the singing of the national anthem, play got under way. The action seemed slow and dull, and time after time Searle's gaze wandered toward the tall, tanned figure in right field. Trying to study Carlton without being obvious, she had to admit the white uniform with the vivid blue stripes looked great stretched across his muscular form.

The muscles of his firm thighs alone were more than Norm Kraekor had in his whole body, she thought irrepressibly. Try as she might, Searle could not stop herself from wondering what that hard, toned body would feel like against hers. With a start, she realized the impact of her thoughts and forced herself to look away from right field.

Letting her eyes travel around the stadium, Searle tried to figure out why people found baseball so interesting. Age didn't seem to be a factor in the sport's attraction, as gray-haired senior citizens yelled with the same fervor of young children. Sex didn't figure either, thought Searle, watching two middle-aged women jump up and down when the third out was called against the opposing team. In fact, she discovered that everyone she saw was having fun. She wondered why. Even the men sitting beside her had forgotten her sensual appeal, she realized wryly, in their spirited enjoyment of the game.

The game recaptured her full attention when Buck Carlton stepped into the batter's box. He was third in the lineup; his two teammates preceding him had quickly been put out. As he took up his stance, Buck cast her a knowing grin and Searle remembered his saucy promise to hit a home run for her. Her long fingers curled around her program and she sat forward attentively. Would he?

Carlton grounded out with a simple line drive to first. The computerized scoreboard flashed a sign, "Batter Luck Next Time," and the next inning began. When he was in the field, Searle's eyes followed the agile movement of the right fielder; when he was sitting in the dugout, out of sight, she tapped her fingers impatiently against her knee. His next two times up at bat, Carlton got on base, but failed to hit the promised homer. Searle derived a smug satisfaction in this, as if it proved he could not bend things so easily to his will.

The game was tied, 2–2, when in the bottom of the ninth

Buck Carlton came to the plate with one man on first and two outs. The crowd howled its desire for a victory. Searle's face was as intent as any other fan's as she watched the strong arms swing the bat toward the first pitch. The ball sailed out over the Blues' emblem and into the dark night. Carlton flashed her the thumbs-up sign as he trotted toward first in his parade of the bases. She felt a sudden quivering. There had been something almost threatening in that victorious gesture of Carlton's. Certainly, she knew it to be something dangerous.

The crowds were clearing swiftly and still Searle hesitated, uncertain what she should do. A glance at her watch told her it was after ten; she really ought to go home and get to sleep. But she had stayed through the game to finish her interview, hadn't she? Just as she decided on home and bed and began to follow the disappearing stream of fans, a voice checked her.

"Would you please follow me, Miss Delacorte?"

She recognized her young usher-escort, and with the feeling of a lamb being led to slaughter, she followed him. He returned her to the small conference room she'd been in before. It appeared Carlton indeed meant to conduct the interview like a professional and Searle ignored the quite unexplainable disappointment that shot through her. She sat and placed her notebook and pen before her, then crossed her legs and waited.

Twenty minutes passed before the door opened, but she forgot how long it had been when she met the warmth that lit Buck's brown eyes as he saw her sitting there, one shapely leg resting on the other. He'd obviously come straight from the showers. His blond hair looked darker, wet curls plastered against his forehead, making him appear absurdly boyish. The white shirt stood out against his deep tan and Searle tried not to notice that he'd buttoned it only halfway up. He was stuffing the ends of the shirt into his denim jeans even as he spoke.

"What'd you think of the game?" he asked, smiling exultantly. He filled the small room with his vibrant energy. Searle was determined not to be overwhelmed.

"I thought, Mr. Carlton, it was every bit as boring as I had expected it to be." Neither the frosty tone nor the cool gaze accompanying it dampened his spirits.

"You'll learn to like it, Searle," he said. His assumption and all that it implied enraged her. She sat stiffly erect, but before she could favor him with her views on his overbearing and thoroughly mistaken attitude, Buck collected her notebook and pen. "Come on, let's go get something to eat. I'm starved."

He'd taken possession of her hand and lifted her from the chair before she squawked, "But the interview!"

"We'll work on it on the way. Hitting homers for beautiful, bored ladies is hungry work."

"I am not hungry, Mr. Carlton," she said as he swept her through the narrow passageway.

He halted abruptly. "Look, call me Buck, okay? Just try it, you'll find it's not so hard. Come on, say it. Buck."

He was smiling. Did he always smile at a woman like that? she wondered. As if he were about to devour her with those passionate lips? She saw the flicker of impatience in the deep eyes and said stubbornly, "No matter what I call you, it doesn't change the fact that I'm not hungry. Besides, I can't conduct an interview in a restaurant."

"Who said anything about a restaurant? And if you won't call me Buck, at least stop giving me this cold Mr. Carlton treatment or there won't be any interview." He thrust open the door and drew her into the cool night air.

Searle gulped at the passing breeze. The threatening closeness of him and the invitingly clean masculine smell of him had both frightened and thrilled her. It was as if he had touched a button no one else had ever seen and turned on a sensitivity even Searle hadn't suspected she possessed.

"Where's your car?" he asked.

"Over there." Searle pointed to her Toyota, standing alone in the near-empty parking lot.

They crossed in silence to the car. She couldn't bring herself to inquire where he meant for them to go, feeling that to do so would prove his command of the situation. As they neared the small white car, Buck paused, hand outstretched. Searle ran her eyes from the open palm to the broad, friendly grin above it. Reaching into her purse, she extracted her keys, hesitated briefly, then gave in to the inevitable and dropped them into his hand.

"Is this your macho thing—can't let a woman drive her own car?" she asked sarcastically, stalking to the passenger side.

Buck eased his large frame into the driver's seat, rolling it back to its utmost limit, before unlocking and flipping open her door. "I think it's more of a defensive thing," he replied easily. "I just don't trust anyone else's driving."

"Don't you have your own car here?" she questioned as they pulled out onto the road.

"Usually, but as it happens my car's in the shop. I rode over to the stadium today with Joey Howe."

"Oh? And I suppose you demanded to drive *his* car?" she prodded.

He laughed, a low, rumbling laugh that invited her to join in. Searle resisted the invitation.

"Where do you live, Searle?" He turned to face her as he stopped at the intersection. "Do I go left or right?"

"*You* do not go to my place," she responded tartly.

"Okay." He turned the Toyota left and expertly eased onto the freeway.

"Where are we going?" she demanded.

"I figure we'll go to my place since you'd rather not go home yet."

"I'd rather not go to your place, either. This is supposed to be an interview, not a . . ." She managed to bite off the word "seduction" just in time. She was determined not to let him understand the effect he was having on her.

"Yes?" he prompted, grinning knowingly.

"Not a dinner date," she finished lamely.

"At my place—or yours," he said pointedly, "we could talk without distraction and I could feed my face, too. And it's a hungry face, Searle." The look he sent her made her very glad she was sitting down. She was certain her legs wouldn't be able to hold her up if he continued to look at her in just that sensual way. She thought quickly and decided she would far rather confront him on her grounds than on his.

"All right. You've got a point. Let's go to my apartment," she said in a voice completely free of the inner upheaval she was experiencing. "As it happens, I live off the next exit."

"Terrific. That means we're not very far from each other. My home's on the edge of Stillwater Lake, you know."

For the sake of her own peace of mind as well as of the interview, Searle asked him to tell her about the game from his point of view, and they passed the rest of the short drive to her apartment complex in a review of the team's play. Listening to him critically analyze the action, she was forced to revise her first impression of the player. Obviously, Buck Carlton had brains in addition to brawn. At the back of her mind, though, was a disquieting question: How had this jock managed to talk her into inviting him up to her place? And what in the world was going to happen next?

CHAPTER THREE

Still wondering what she had done, was doing, Searle slipped her key in the lock of her second-floor apartment. Flicking a switch as she passed through the door, she did not look to see Buck follow her in, but advanced into the room, casually dropping her purse onto the smoked glass top of a low chrome table. The closing of the door sounded behind her with an ominous finality. Neither spoke as Searle continued on into her tiny kitchenette. Bright light flooded the narrow rectangle in harsh contrast to the soft circle of lamplight casting shadows over Buck in the living room.

Arms akimbo, he slowly revolved, letting his eyes stroll over the room. A beige sofa and chair were placed against opposite walls, a white ceramic lamp with cream shade stood on the glass table beside the chair. On the matching glass and chrome coffee table lay a copy of *Smithsonian,* while one utilitarian bookcase housed neat rows of books. It might have been, thought Buck with a shake of his head, a model room for show. Certainly no one could live in such antiseptic precision.

Glancing across the tiled counter that separated the cooking nook from the living room, Buck watched as Searle measured ground coffee into a drip machine. The liquid sensuality of her commonplace movements stirred the craving he'd felt from the moment he had seen her. It wasn't that she was beautiful. Buck had had plenty of beautiful women, and beauty by itself meant little to him. It was the enigma of her that intrigued him. The passionate invitation she issued with every movement of her graceful body was utterly revoked by her unapproachable air of detachment. To him, Searle was like a deep red rose kept behind a sheet of glass. No one could touch the velvety softness of her hidden petals, no one could bring to bloom the promise of her unopened bud.

Returning his gaze to the white-on-white quilted picture of a wave cresting that hung above her couch, he at last spoke.

"I can see that what you need is some color in your life."

"Oh?" said Searle without looking at him. She felt vividly conscious of him. Even his smallest movement jarred her senses, and because she didn't normally respond to men in this way, Searle felt unusually jittery. The feeling irritated her. Clattering coffee cups into saucers, she asked tartly, "Any particular shades?"

"Blues," he responded instantly. "One certain Blue, to be exact," he added with another of his virile grins.

Ignoring this, Searle poured dark, steaming liquid into the cups, then set them on the countertop. Leaning slightly forward in a manner that Carlton considered highly provocative, she asked coolly, "So what do you want?"

The sudden desire flaming in the soft sable of his eyes told her more surely than any words. Buck stood still, consuming her with his heated gaze. "I want—" he began huskily.

"I mean to *eat,*" she interrupted hurriedly.

A sudden smile curved under his moustache. Before she could blink, both smile and moustache had materialized in the kitchenette beside her. Though fairly tall herself, Searle felt dwarfed beside the massive form crowding the narrow space. A ridiculous need to escape his overwhelming presence swept over her, but she kept a firm rein on her jumpy nerves. This was, she sternly reminded herself, just an interview.

"Let's see what you've got," said Buck cheerfully. His hands lightly took possession of her curved hips; with one agile motion, he reversed their positions within the thin strip of walking space. He plunged into the refrigerator while Searle, seemingly disinterested, watched. Inside her, a series of unexpected, unknown tingles were transmitting themselves from her hips to her heart. *My God,* she thought unsteadily, *my God!*

"My God," swore Buck, causing her to jump. "How do you manage to live? I can't find anything but yogurt and fruit."

Searle had no intention of letting this jock realize his unnerving effect. Tapping her well-established reserve, she produced a practiced, chilling smile. "I didn't expect a dinner guest," she said dampingly. "There are eggs on the lower shelf and vegetables in the bin, but I've not thawed out any meat."

Shutting the door, he shrugged philosophically. "You got any bread, peanut butter?"

Thinking this was exactly the kind of taste she expected of him, Searle wordlessly extracted the requested items from a cupboard while Buck's head disappeared again into the depths of the fridge. He withdrew triumphantly a few seconds later with a butter dish and a jar of pickles. He yanked a small frying pan from its hook on the pegboard covering the meager width of wall between the stove and refrigerator, then slapped it onto a burner.

"What are you making?" asked Searle, eyeing these maneuvers with lukewarm interest.

"A rare delicacy, a delight that's been handed from father to son in the Carlton family," he replied with a grand flourish of a slice of bread liberally spread with peanut butter. He pressed two slices together, dotted butter on them, then plopped the concoction into the pan. "You're about to discover the pleasures of the grilled peanut butter sandwich," he declared.

"So being a gourmet is added to your list of accomplishments," remarked Searle with cool cynicism.

"Just wait 'til you've tasted it to criticize, lady," returned her unperturbed chef. "Slice some pickles and get us some plates."

"Pickles? With peanut butter?"

"Don't scoff until you've tried it. I suppose you were one of those finicky children who never ate anything that looked or sounded odd. You miss a lot that way, Searle."

The mildly paternal tone offended her. She clapped a pair of plates on the counter, then stalked around the corner to claim one of the high chrome stools. Sipping her coffee, she berated herself for letting him come to her apartment. His dominating manner disturbed her and she definitely did not like being ruffled this way. She was actually struggling to retain her composure—something she had not had to do in a very long time.

Her fingers tattooed the countertop. Searle watched them closely, not daring to look at the man responsible for her agitation. A plate whipped into place at her elbow. She glanced from it to Buck, dismayed. "But I'm not hungry," she protested.

"You can't make disparaging remarks about my culinary talents with impunity. Besides, you need to eat. You're too thin."

Did this big lump ever take no for an answer? she wondered in disgust. Never, never had she been steamrollered this way. And worse, she thought wryly, there were moments she found herself enjoying it. She bit into the gooey sandwich. It was surprisingly good.

"Good, but it sticks," she mumbled through the melted peanut butter.

"That's what the pickle's for. Take a bite," he ordered as he came around, plate in hand, to join her at the counter.

The pickle juice offset the goo of the sandwich, and somehow added to the flavor. It not only tasted good, it stimulated her appetite. She ate the whole concoction quickly, smiling as she crunched down the last of the pickle.

"What did I tell you?" inquired Buck with satisfaction. He watched in appreciation as she slipped from the stool and returned to the kitchen. She replenished her cup with more coffee, then quickly rinsed her plate and placed it into the dishwasher. None of this surprised him; the bare perfection of her apartment told him she would put everything in its place. People, too, if she could. "Well," he said as he licked remnants of his sandwich from his moustache, "what do you want to know about me?"

She looked directly at him and, fascinated, Buck saw her lower lip thrust outward, then slide up into a smile that took his breath away. Before he had recovered, she had retrieved her purse, collected her notebook from within it, and repositioned herself on the stool beside him.

"I need background," she said in her businesslike clip. "Is Buck your real name?" In quick response to his raised brow, she added defensively, "No, I didn't do my homework. To be honest, I couldn't see wasting my time on a story about a jock."

His sandy brows rose higher at her frankness. "You really dislike me, don't you?" he probed in an expressionless voice.

Searle examined the squared face, noticing creases tracking beside his dark, almond-shaped eyes. Lines from looking into the sun? From laughing at life? She didn't know and she didn't want to know, she reminded herself.

"No, I don't dislike you," she answered as she moved her eyes back to her notebook. "I'm not too crazy about this assignment, that's all. I'm not a sportswriter and I don't aspire to be one."

"So it's sports in general you dislike."

"I find games to be a silly waste of time. But it doesn't matter what I think, does it?" She punctuated her question with a coolly arched brow. Buck wondered if she ever warmed up to anything or anyone. It would be a crime for her to pass through life without experiencing its warmth.

"No, I guess not, just so you don't move your dislike from the general to the specific," he replied slowly.

Searle had been the object of more than her share of bedroom eyes, but the dark glitter beneath Buck's half-lowered lids held something more. All too aware of his masculine proximity, she raised her pen over her pad like some ancient gladiator raising a shield before the lions. "Your name?" she prompted brusquely.

"Carlton."

"Yes, I know," she said shortly. "I meant your first name."

"Carlton," he repeated. As her head jerked up, cat's eyes seeming to slant farther upward in anger, he explained with an apologetic shrug, "There's not much imagination in my family. I'm not even the first Carlton Carlton. My grandfather had that peculiar honor."

"So you were named for your grandfather?"

"No, for my father." There was now a distinct twinkle in the coffee eyes. "He was Carlton Carlton, Junior. That's what he was always called, Junior. So when I came along, in their overabundance of Carltons, they called me Buck. No reason that I know of, but Buck is what I've always been."

Firm, precise little notes were entered into her notebook. As she scribbled, her full lower lip advanced outward, tempting Buck to capture its softness with his own lips. Resisting this, he inquired lightly, "And where did you get a name like Searle? Is it for real?"

Looking up, Searle saw his gaze fastened on her mouth and knew an absurd moment of panic. What was it about this guy that he, of all men, could so easily penetrate all her cultivated self-preserving indifference at a glance? Maintaining an impersonal note through sheer force of will, she stated calmly, "I think we've established that this is your interview, not mine. What do you think is behind your success?"

"Ability," he replied, accepting her retreat with a grin. "In baseball, or any sport for that matter, ability transcends all other considerations. But I also stay calm in a tight situation—however many strikes, however many outs, I don't choke up." His eyes slid over her. "Remember that, Searle, I don't choke."

There was a message for her in that look, but Searle firmly ignored it. "Tell me, what is it you want out of life?" she asked. "Life after baseball."

"What every other guy wants, I guess. A home, a family." He saw the disbelief cross her svelte features and added dryly, "Jocks need love, too, Searle."

"But the stay-at-home-family-man image doesn't quite fit with the playboy athlete who squires models and showgirls in and out of his life with machine-gun rapidity," she pointed out, restlessly tapping her pen on her pad.

"That's only because I hadn't yet found the woman for me," he explained in a tone that brought her head up. "The media labels any guy who isn't married and dates around a playboy, automatically precluding the idea of a desire for a lasting relationship. But I've wanted marriage. For me, it had to be with the right woman. And up to now, I've just been looking."

Skepticism plainly stamped Searle's face, but Buck was arrested by something more, something he couldn't define, that mingled there. "Don't you want marriage, Searle? A commitment to share life with Mr. Right?"

"No!" she answered explosively. Astonished brown eyes stared into astonished green. Then Searle turned her head away and composed herself while brushing back a stray strand of hair that had escaped the roll. "I don't believe Cinderella always finds Prince Charming. With the divorce rate as high as it is, I don't see how anyone can.

But," she said emphatically as she stood, "that's neither here nor there. More coffee?"

Taking his cup before he could respond, Searle retreated to the safety of the brightly lit kitchenette. She poured out a cupful, then slid it toward him. As he took the cup, she picked up his empty plate. She was placing it into the dishwasher when he came up behind her.

"So you don't believe in marriage?" he questioned.

"It's not for everyone," she replied flatly.

"Meaning, it's not for you," he suggested.

She did not answer, concentrating on the handle of the dishwasher. He watched her terse, tense movements for a time, then inquired, "So tell me, what's so awful about marriage?"

"It smothers individuality," she said after a pause, her voice sounding rusty to her own ears, "especially for women."

"Ahhh," responded Buck on a drawn-out breath.

She looked sharply at him then. "What's that mean?"

"You're a feminist," he explained in tones that rankled Searle to her depths. "You believe all that male-domination crap."

"What I am," returned Searle through her teeth, "is a realist. Too many people make a bad job of marriage—and I don't believe in making a bad job of anything."

His open grin annoyed her. She turned her attention to the frying pan and spatula, placing them in the sink.

"Well, do you believe in fooling around?" he lightly queried, leaning slightly closer. Both his tone and the gleam in his eye were nothing less than highly suggestive and Searle chose to ignore him.

She filled the pan with soap and water, busying herself with washing it. He took a linen towel from the rod on the door below the sink, his arm grazing her leg as he did so. The electricity of his brief touch froze her for a bare instant, then, as he stood waiting, she quickly finished washing and rinsing the pan. Handing it to him, careful not to touch him, she said evenly, "The female readers of *Our Town* will certainly be interested to know what kind of woman you're looking for."

"Oh, but I'm not looking," Buck denied breezily as he handed the dried pan back to her.

Grateful that he couldn't see her face, Searle hung the pan on the pegboard hook at the end of the narrow kitchen nook. "But I thought you said you have been."

"That was before I discovered that all the looking in the world doesn't do any good." He stepped close behind her; turning, Searle found herself completely trapped by him. Placing both hands on the board behind her, one on either side of her head, Buck continued in a voice suddenly sensuously low. "Looking for love isn't the answer. It's something that just happens, unbidden, unexpected. If you're lucky, you're ready for it. Are you ready, Searle?" he murmured thickly.

His breath laid softly upon her cheeks. She had tilted her head back in order to look at him, and she now lowered her lids to shut out the bruising intensity of his deep chocolate eyes. He mistook her action; her only warning was the heat of his breath preceding his lips upon hers. Her mouth was pillowy soft beneath the insistent pressure of his.

Alarm bells sounded a warning in her head and for just an instant, Searle wanted to ignore them, wanted to go on enjoying the exciting touch of his lips, the downy tickle of his moustache. But the alarms clamored to be heard and years of habit die hard. Feeling slightly dizzy, she brought her hands up to push blindly against his rock-hard chest.

Buck did not, at first, seem inclined to respond, but Searle persisted, her increasing withdrawal communicating itself clearly to him, and he reluctantly pulled his mouth away from hers. Still keeping her locked within his hold, he asked in a hoarse whisper, "What is it?"

"I—please—this isn't the way to conduct an interview," she insisted, contriving to keep her voice even, though her breath was ragged.

"But it wasn't an interview I was thinking of conducting," he countered, tightening his grip to press her closer into his muscled contours.

Feeling the hard warmth of his desire, Searle experienced a sudden wave of shock. The matching surge of need rising within her both agitated and appalled her. Afraid to face up to the torrent of inflaming sensations engulfing her, she forced her eyes to open, forced herself to meet Buck's ardent gaze. Dumbfounded, she recognized the hint of amusement threaded through the dark passion glinting in his eyes. Resentment exploded within her. Her senses felt as if they'd been run through all ten speeds of an emotional blender and the big moose responsible for it stood calmly, maddeningly pleased with himself.

Shoving forcefully, she freed herself from his grasp and strode angrily from the kitchen. She felt as foolish as someone caught without any clothes on. As Buck followed her, she whirled and inquired in arctic accents, "Tell me, is this the way you jocks play the game? Meet 'em and mate 'em in one inning?"

The amusement she had suspected glimmering in his eyes now lifted the tanned creases beside them and extended to the ends of his moustache. That he should laugh at her only outraged Searle further and with a flair of high drama any actress would envy, she threw her arm out and pointed to the door.

"If you do not mind, Mr. Carlton," she snapped, "I must go to bed!"

"Is this an invitation?" he inquired with a crooked smile that earned him a fulminating frown.

"This is an invitation for you to leave," she enunciated bitingly.

He went obediently, meekly toward the door. Searle could have stamped her foot in rage. Then, with his hand on the knob, Buck turned.

"You should have remembered the old adage, lady," he said. "If you can't take the heat, stay out of the kitchen." With a wide grin, he was gone.

CHAPTER FOUR

The coffeemaker produced its regular small pot, but the cup Searle had poured sat untouched beside the unread morning paper. She stood, uncharacteristically dreamy, before the double glass doors overlooking her square patch of patio.

Every word, every pause of last night reechoed through her mind. It was not, on the whole, pleasant reflection. With distaste, Searle recalled the unexpected, unwanted, unexplainable yearnings Buck Carlton had aroused in her, yearnings that had lasted long after he left. She had not liked being so sexually aware of him. It had disturbed her; more, it had alarmed her and she'd struck out in defensive anger. She felt a twinge of anger now and told herself emphatically that Buck Carlton and Searle Delacorte definitely were not meant for each other.

Searle knew only too well what could result from the pairing of two such mismatched people. She had no intention of stepping willingly into the trap—hadn't she guarded against it since she had been old enough to understand the consequences of an unhappy marriage?

She had watched her parents pick each other apart until all that had been best and good in each disintegrated in the mutual desire to wound, again and again. The constant bickering and frequent violent explosions formed Searle's early resolution not to expose herself to such torment. Any danger of heartache was rendered unlikely by the deliberate numbing of her own emotions. Shielded by her glacial indifference, Searle had suffered no pain at the hands of any man; many, in fact, had termed her frigid, in need of mental counseling. But she had continued on, secure in her belief that hers was the only intelligent way to get through life. It had been both her fortune and her misfortune that no man had appeared to pierce through the heavy armor of her reserve.

Until now.

Now there was Buck Carlton. For Searle, it could not have been worse. They were complete opposites, without the least common denominator between them. Like a too-vivid nightmare, she could clearly picture the result of any relationship between them. Just as with her parents, there would be the initial attempts to change one another, followed by the inevitable disappointments, and finally, the rage and disgust.

A jock! her mind fairly shouted. Why did she have to be attracted to some overmacho jock?

Searle would always prefer a painful truth to a sweet lie. With aching honesty, she admitted the physical attraction; more, she admitted her fear of it. Although, at twenty-five, she could be termed "experienced" in the matter of sex, she had never had experience with desire. That she had, however briefly, wanted Buck Carlton to go on kissing her, touching her, had shaken her confidence badly. The last thing she wanted was to end like her mother—bitter, hateful, literally eaten up with jealous spite.

Though Buck claimed to be a victim of media labeling, Searle did not believe this. As a journalist, she knew that each story had a foundation; Buck's womanizing reputation had not sprung from the mind of an overzealous newsman. She recognized the protestations of innocence, of a desire for a homelife, for the fantasy they were. Hadn't she heard her father brush aside numerous affairs with the same protests often enough to know this?

Much better, much safer to go through life on an even plane of nonemotion. Much better. She had conquered her inexplicable feelings toward Carlton last night and she would go on conquering them.

Turning away from the window, Searle swore softly as

she caught sight of her large-faced wall clock. Moving with quick grace, she dumped her cold coffee down the sink, rinsed her cup, and turned off the maker. She'd have to clean it out later. She hated leaving dirty dishes and this only added to her chafed mood. As she dashed down the steps to the parking lot, she resolved to have it out with Lenn this morning. Somehow she would make him understand that she simply could not do this Carlton story.

The drive was an easy one, for Searle knew every dip and bend, the nuances of the freeway as familiar to her as her own apartment. She let her mind wander, trying to channel her thoughts into soothing directions, but invariably they came back to the man who had so precipitously disrupted her ordered existence.

Buck Carlton was the epitome of what Searle considered distasteful in a man. When she desired male companionship, which was only rarely, she admitted, she liked her men polished, cultivated, cool—the kind of man whose masculinity was subordinate to his personality. The earthy Carlton oozed a supreme kind of masculinity, the kind that always took what was wanted and casually left behind what was not. His boyish charm would appeal to many women, she supposed, but she definitely was not among them. This was simply a foolish physical attraction that she would do well to put out of her mind—now.

But the firmest of resolutions failed to dispel the image of sun-kissed golden hair, laughing brown eyes, and firmly toned, tanned muscles. She shook her head slightly as if to wipe out the image lodged there, and fixed her gaze on the distant skyline.

On a day like today when the city stood proudly against the crystalline backdrop of the summer sky, appreciation for the beauty of it drove all other considerations from her mind. There was something impressive in man's determination to reach for the sky with bigger, bolder buildings, something Searle admired. By the time she guided her car into the Midwest lot, she felt composed and more than ready to tackle Lenn Roberts.

Without pausing to check in with the receptionist, Searle went directly to the editor's office. His door stood open; the unlit office was empty. Illuminating the room with fluorescent light, she entered and sat down to wait. She was straightening the folds of her lightweight linen dress when he came in. Roberts halted, looked her up and down, then quite deliberately made a show of removing the jacket of his seersucker suit, hanging it neatly behind the door. Adjusting the fit of his vest, he moved leisurely to claim his chair.

"To what do I owe this unexpected pleasure?" he asked at last.

"It's the Buck Carlton story," answered Searle succinctly.

Leaning back, Roberts arched his hands fingertip to fingertip. Contemplating them as if they held the secrets to the universe, he mildly said, "Oh?"

"I can't do it," she said with flat resolution.

"You astound me." Lenn bounced his fingers together. "The last words I ever expected from you, Searle, were 'I can't.' Do you perhaps mean, you won't?"

A brief flinch sketched over her features, then Searle explained calmly, "It's not a matter of semantics, Lenn. I simply don't feel capable of handling this story. I want off. Now."

"And, as I told you yesterday, I haven't got another writer to do it." The editor's hands dropped to the desk as he leaned forward. "What did you get yesterday?"

"A big zero." Searle stood and began pacing, a restless gesture that surprised Roberts. "He took control of the interview and I let him run away with it. Lenn, these macho types are beyond me."

There was an astonishing pleading note. With a frown, Lenn again shook his head. "I'm sorry, but—"

"But I really don't want to do it!" cut in Searle sharply.

A shocked silence held the two for several seconds. Then, scanning the stony determination on Searle's lovely, asymmetrical face, Roberts tranquilly inquired of the air, "I wonder what has become of my passionless professional?"

"Don't be patronizing!" she snapped, jerking to a stop before his desk to glare at him.

Raising his silvery brows above the gold rim of his glasses, Lenn said calmly, "I wasn't. Look, Searle, we've already lined up scores of advertisers for that issue simply on the basis of the Carlton feature, and there's been some spillover into the papers. We can't afford to lose ad dollars simply because you don't feel you want to do the story."

Inwardly, Searle sighed. Of course she'd have to do it. Ad dollars meant profits and that meant everything with the men at the top. She stared into his faded blue eyes for only a moment more, then said through tight lips, "Oh, very well, I'll finish your damned feature."

She heard Lenn's chuckle as she strode out, and it rankled all the way back to her cubicle office. The company was coming awake with sound and light as people arrived, but Searle was only dimly aware of the activity around her. She would finish the article on Carlton—she was a professional, wasn't she? She would simply have to give the big jock the coldest shoulder this side of Antarctica to do it.

Flinging open her office door, Searle stopped dead at the threshold. Standing on the center of her desk, overflowing its minimal space, was an abundant profusion of vibrant flowers. Entering and closing the door, she realized she was trembling. *How odd,* thought Searle in passing, *men usually send me roses.* She saw carnations, daisies, mums, and all sorts of flowers she couldn't lay a name to; varying shades of yellows, blues, pinks, and even white gave the arrangement a kaleidoscopic effect as she slowly turned the green cut-glass bowl around. She found a card tucked within the greenery and, inhaling deeply, opened it with shaking fingers.

Each petal is a gift of color. No name. But Searle knew, of course, that they could only be from Buck. How on earth had he managed it at this hour of the morning? She eyed the bouquet again with the wary look of an animal confronting its worst predator. She thought she should dump the whole thing into the trash immediately. Instead, she pushed her clump of ivy to the back of her file cabinet and very carefully placed the colorful bouquet beside it. It wouldn't do any harm to keep the flowers, she told herself. They livened the place up.

Collecting her much abused notebook and pen, Searle marched off to the company morgue and dove into the library's backlog of sports pages. Two hours later she had the background on Buck Carlton completed with an efficient thoroughness that was her trademark. *Only his mother could possibly know more about him,* she thought with a satisfied smile as she returned to her office, her earlier displeasure completely gone.

She was in the middle of typing up her notes when the phone rang. Grabbing the receiver with one quick hand, she cradled it between her ear and shoulder, continuing to type. "Umm, Delacorte," she said absently.

"Umm, Delacorte, how are ya?" laughed a husky male voice.

The clacking of the typewriter stopped abruptly. For a long instant Searle hesitated before she managed evenly, "Oh. Hello, Buck."

"Such warmth," he remarked in dry tones. "Do you always greet people with such enthusiasm?"

There was another pause. Searle heard her heart thump loudly and ridiculously hoped he could not hear it, too.

"Did you like them?" he asked finally, almost brusquely.

"Like what?" she returned, knowing full well what.

"I thought you didn't like playing games," said Buck, just a shade cynically. "The flowers."

"Oh. Yes, thank you, they're lovely," responded Searle in a careful voice of distant politeness. "I can't imagine how you managed to get them delivered so early."

"It helps to have a connection," he explained shortly. "A close friend runs a flower shop and she took care of it for me."

She. Close friend. Now why the hell had her heart suddenly shifted into low gear? Not understanding what was happening to her composure, she repeated woodenly, "Oh, well, thank you."

"Do me a favor, will you?" Buck asked with a sudden change of tone.

"What?" she parried cautiously.

"Wear your hair down for tonight's game. I'd like to see you looking something other than beautifully efficient. Simply beautiful will do just fine."

The audacity of it took her breath away. With smooth control, Searle gave him to understand that how he would like to see her was of no importance. "I do not intend to be at the game tonight in any case," she finished coolly.

"Sure you do. I've got your seat reserved for you," he pointed out with a confidence that made Searle's hand clench into a fist. This guy obviously expected every woman to fall flat at his feet! "I thought maybe tonight we'd try my place," he continued cheerfully. "The atmosphere might not be as classy, but the larder is better stocked."

"Try to understand, Mr. Carlton—"

"Buck."

"That we are not going out tonight," said Searle through tight lips. "We are not going out at all. Our relationship—"

"Well, that's better," he cut in on a note of approval. "At least you admit we have one."

"The relationship is strictly business!" she spit out.

"Some business," he murmured. On her sharp intake of breath, Buck added, "Look, you couldn't have gotten enough out of me for a story last night and I really would like to cooperate with the hometown mag. I won't be able to see you before the game—I'm locked up with a TV interview—but after the game we'll talk. Be there, Searle."

His soft tone was very persuasive. Searle held her breath, thinking remotely that she ought to hang up.

"Searle?" he said.

"Yes?" she responded without inflection.

"Don't worry about your hair. If you wear it up, I'll just have the fun of taking it down later."

With a click that was as boldly assured as he had been, Buck hung up. Holding the phone for a full ten seconds more, Searle stared accusingly at the flowers. See what you have done? she seemed to demand of the bouquet. Dropping the receiver into its cradle, she propped her chin on her hands and considered the impertinence of Mr. Carlton Carlton the Third.

The man was a bit like a bulldozer going through a pile of sand. Used to getting what he wanted, Buck had the confidence to make him the envy of everyone who ever took a self-assertiveness course. Especially, thought Searle with a tinge of disgust, where women were concerned. She easily understood why. Behind his engaging charm lay a potent sexuality that drugged the senses with a glance. His ability to look at a woman as if she were the only object on earth must have gotten him everywhere. Well, ol' Bucky was due for a surprise. He was about to discover that this sandpile had a foundation of steel.

She would, of course, go to the game. She'd told Lenn she'd finish the feature and she would. It would be the best damn piece she'd ever done, too. And she just might enjoy being the woman who put Buck Carlton firmly in his place. She would do so by calling upon all the defenses she'd learned over the years. She promised herself that she would resist his heady charm, she would remain detached. Though he had already made her violently angry, there would be no further such displays. She would stay calm, poised, remote.

These resolutions were still in her mind as Searle searched her closet that evening. Early in her teens, she had discovered that dressing with a certain high style made men approach her more cautiously than they did her more casual friends. She'd learned the lesson well, and though her selection of clothes was not large, every item had a sophisticated elegance that added to her image. For the first time in her life, though, she stood staring into the orderly rack of clothes and wished for a pair of jeans.

She finally chose a pair of lavender silk slacks and a deep lilac silk camisole, with a wide bronze belt and heeled sandals to match. Standing before the full-length mirror hung on the back of her bedroom door, she sighed. She looked good, but she knew she'd be overdressed. At least for the game, she thought wryly. Raising her hands to the twist of hair pinned securely in place, Searle hesitated. Then, firmly, she turned from the mirror. Really, she scolded herself, he must not be allowed to dictate these things!

A glance at the slim gold watch on her wrist told her it was time to go. A thrill of excited anticipation shot through her, but she appeared as aloofly self-possessed as ever as she swung the strap of her purse over her bare shoulder and strode to her car.

At the ball park, there was no wait when she presented her *Our Town* ID to the gatekeeper. She was led directly and cordially to a field box seat. This time, however, it was on the third-baseline and provided a perfect view into the Blues' dugout. She discovered this as, turning from thanking her escort, she looked to her right and directly into the broadly grinning face of the Blues' right fielder.

Even at this distance, she could see the satisfaction stamped over the tanned, square features. He lifted a hand in acknowledgment of her presence. Without responding, Searle removed her eyes, apparently studying the program with avid interest. She did not see the widening effect this had on Buck's grin; nor did she see the page of the program she was examining so intently. All she could see was Carlton's smug self-assurance. No wonder he always looks so confident, her mind hissed at her. He thinks all he has to do is lift his finger and women appear. He'd soon learn she wasn't the easiest thing walking the earth on two legs!

Easy was not the word Buck would have used. Behind the satisfaction, he'd felt real pleasure at seeing Searle arrive. He had spent the afternoon planning what to do if she didn't show up, and seeing her now filled him with a surge of desire he had never known with any other woman. Gazing at her during the whole of the national anthem, he pondered the challenge she presented. He didn't know why she hid from life behind the frosty facade, but he damn well intended to find out. He wanted the woman he suspected Searle was to come out into the open. The jaunty smile he flashed at her as the music came to an end with a reverberating shout of "Play ball" was met with an answering stiff politeness that reinforced his determination to get through to her.

Broadcasters ran out of superlatives for the way Buck Carlton played the game. He quickly followed a solid single with two triples, the second of which sent his overall average over the magic .400 mark and sent the fans into a howling, cheering, stamping frenzy. Searle found herself on her feet as the fans demanded acknowledgment from Carlton. Standing on third, his expression clearly visible to her, Buck doffed his cap to the public and smiled directly at Searle.

It was Carlton's night, the announcers all agreed, as late in the game he made an incredible leaping catch that nearly sent him into the stands and robbed the opposing team of a home run. That the Blues won the game seemed to matter little; Buck Carlton was the man of the hour. Even as the last out was trapped in a glove, media hounds were gathering to encircle him. Buck was carried away on the tide of their flooding questions, and Searle, seeing him disappear from view, puzzled over what she should do.

Thinking at first that she would wait, she was startled when a young boy in a miniature Blues' uniform dashed across the field toward her.

"Miss Delacorte?" he asked, tilting his head back to look up at her.

"Yes," she said, leaning over the rail to meet his earnest eyes.

"Mr. Carlton told me to tell you to wait for him. If you'd like to go through the concourse, I'll meet you and—"

"What exactly did Mr. Carlton say?" she cut in, looking like a magnificent cold goddess to the young boy.

"Gee, miss, he just said 'Tell her she's to wait,' " he explained.

"I see." She did see. She saw that Buck Carlton thought he could simply order her here, order her there. "You may tell Mr. Carlton," she said sweetly, very sweetly, "that I had other plans for this evening."

She left before the bat boy could protest. Wow, he thought, he didn't want to tell Buck Carlton *that!*

Anger kept her company all the way home. She didn't stop to remember that she had promised herself not to let Buck affect her least emotion; she only remembered the cocksure look of satisfaction on his face whenever their eyes had caught during the night. Which was, she recalled stonily, a damned sight too often!

Well-schooled in the art of suppressing her emotions,

Searle had regained her outward composure by the time she entered her apartment. What she needed, she decided, was a relaxing shower, then a good night's sleep. Neatly hanging up her clothes, placing her shoes in their precise position in her closet, she focused her thoughts on her work, other stories and columns that had to be done before the next deadline. Pulling out her sheer, laced teddy pajamas with the tiny boxed bottoms, she moved into her small bathroom and tested the temperature of the water as she tugged a shower cap over her dark hair.

Searle soon gave herself up to the delicious warmth of the hot spray drumming her back and splashing over her shoulders. She felt the tension draining from her muscles with the water, but as steam clouded the little room, her thoughts turned unwillingly back to Buck.

In the soothing heat of the shower, these thoughts did not unnerve her as much as they had previously. She knew her analysis of Carlton to be accurate. Could she apply the same clinical objectivity to herself? Why had she responded to the male hunger he blatantly displayed? Why did he make her so angry? Turning her face to the spray, letting it play over her cheeks and dance down her firm breasts, Searle faced the inescapable truth.

Her own body inexplicably hungered for his. Despite her best intentions, she had felt it when he'd smiled so triumphantly at her that moment amidst the frenzy of the fans. The smile had been strictly for her and her body had responded with instant, thrilling desire. That, of course, explained her own anger. Although she directed it at him, a good portion of her ill-temper was meant for her own inability to control the need he somehow instilled in her.

People many times overcame such cravings of the body. They overcame the need for alcohol, cigarettes, even sex. This sudden yearning for Buck Carlton could be overcome. The thinking, feeling part of her did not want anything to do with him; she would smother the part of her that did.

Feeling satisfied with her cool rationale, Searle stepped from the shower, freeing her hair from the confines of the wet cap. Shaking the damp from her body like a dog fresh from a swim, she dried, then lightly dusted her shapely curves with a scented powder. Donning her slip-top teddies, she even smiled as she headed for her bed. She would finish the story, hand it in to Lenn, and undoubtedly forget ol' what's-his-name within a week.

The corner of her bedspread was in her hand, about to be dragged back, when the doorbell rang. Searle froze in midmotion, then stared unbelieving toward the living room. The second peremptory chime shook her from her daze and, dropping the cover in disgust, she went to the door. Who would call at such an hour? It was nearly midnight, for pete's sake. As she placed her hand on the lock, she knew who it had to be and experienced a varying range of emotions, not the least of which was a strange, unwelcome elation.

CHAPTER FIVE

Cautiously cracking open her front door, Searle peered around its edge and into the scowling features of Buck Carlton. Without warning, he shoved the door wide.

"What the hell did you mean by—" he began hotly, then broke off abruptly as he turned midway into the room. "Sweet Jesus," he whispered.

The sleek roll of classically precise hair had been replaced by a flowing midnight mane that tumbled in wild abandon over her bare shoulders, highlighting the alabaster gleam of her skin against the deep burgundy of the skimpy lace top. Staring at the well-defined outline of her firm, high breasts, Buck again whispered hoarsely, "Sweet, sweet Jesus."

Stung into action by the piercing desire in his eyes, Searle swept from the room without a word. Her heart was pounding and her legs felt as substantial as water, but she managed to walk with her normal long, sexy strides. She mentally cursed that simply seeing him could affect her so and that the blatant hunger in his eyes should thrill her so much. Firmly, she set her thoughts aside.

Watching the shapely length of her bared legs, the sculpted beauty of her smooth back as she disappeared, Buck drew in a deep breath. Whatever anger he had felt vanished.

In moments, she returned, wearing a long cotton robe. "What do you want?" she inquired with all the warmth of the berg that sank the *Titanic.*

He had been standing in front of the patio doors, staring into the dimly lit parking lot below. Dropping the beige drapes back into place, he pivoted slowly.

"You have got to be the loveliest woman I've ever seen," he said simply.

"Well, if that's what you wanted—"

"What I want, Searle," he interrupted with a sudden return to the humor that deepened the creases by his eyes, "would provide an obscene caller with plenty of material."

She blushed. She could not believe it, but he'd made her flush again, just like some inexperienced high-schooler.

Buck's moustache twitched suspiciously, but he didn't laugh. Instead, he said pleasantly, "What I wanted originally was to wring your slender neck. Why didn't you wait for me?"

Feeling more composed now that he wasn't searing her with that look that caught her breath in her throat, Searle replied placidly, "I could see you would be a long time with all the reporters and newsmen. And as I do have to work tomorrow, I didn't think it would be worth the long wait."

"Boy, you really know how to compliment a guy," he remarked without rancor. "What did you do, take a mail-order course on 'Ten Easy Ways to Deflate a Male Ego'?"

She had fixed her eyes on a spot slightly to the left of his shoulder. At this, her gaze slid to his face, which wore a droll air of martyrdom. Without a flicker of expression, she said simply, "I didn't have to. I wrote the book."

His infectious, full laughter embraced her warmly. "I'll bet you did at that," he agreed. "I'll bet you did."

"Well, as we have settled that earthshaking question," said Searle dispassionately, "let's say good night."

"But we haven't settled anything," he objected.

"Oh? There's something more?"

"Well, there's the date you owe me," answered Buck. He quietly came to stand in front of her.

"I don't owe you anything," she quickly denied, knowing she should step away from him, but somehow unable to move.

"Sure you do. We had a date, you stood me up. Therefore, you owe me one date," he explained in the voice of a teacher explaining that two plus two equals four.

"But we didn't have a date!" protested Searle feebly. The full force of his steamroller technique was having its effect. She felt as if she'd just been running the Boston Marathon.

"Sure we did." Buck stepped closer. Reaching out, he captured a strand of the black hair. Tenderly twisting it around his fingers, he said softly, "I knew it would look like this. Why do you hide such beauty?" Without waiting for an answer, he went on more casually. "Thursday's an off night. We could go out, have a good time."

"You seem to forget," she said somewhat breathlessly, "that the only object of my seeing you at all is to gather information. I'm not interested in having a good time."

"Would you rather indulge in a bad time?" he asked suggestively.

"If you don't mind, I'd like to go to bed—sleep," said Searle, knocking his hand away from her hair and forcing herself to step away.

"I don't mind the least bit. Just tell me when to pick you up Thursday night and I'll leave."

She stared, emerald eyes glinting with an anger she was struggling to control. Buck stood casually in possession of her living room, hands now stuffed into the pockets of his faded jeans, the prison-gray T-shirt stretched tautly across his muscular chest.

"Do you ever," she clipped, "take no for an answer?"

"Not for something I'm determined to have," he answered promptly. "Come on, kid, I'll show you a good time."

If only, she thought with irritation, his damned smile weren't so engaging. "I am not a kid, Mr. Carlton," she said tersely.

"I thought I made it clear you should call me Buck."

"Look, I—"

"Were you always this obstinate?" he broke in on a note of academic interest. "I suppose your parents neglected to spank you during your formative years."

No, they were too busy hitting each other to pay attention to me passed through her mind before she spoke.

"Buck, I don't think . . ." she started.

"She's got it! By George, she's got it!" he cut in with a laugh that caught her off-guard.

Unable to restrain it, an unwanted burble of laughter escaped from her, bringing a dark glow to the sable eyes intently watching her. Searle certainly hadn't wanted to laugh, she told herself she shouldn't, and yet his absurd charm seemed to force it from her.

"You simply do not give up, do you?" she managed through her honeyed laughter.

"Hardly ever. So how about eight? No, let's make it seven—I'll never be able to wait 'til eight to see you." Moving swiftly with a lithe step, he again placed himself before her. Calmly, with masterful deliberation, he ringed the softness of her neck with the roughness of his callused palm. He could feel the erratic coursing of her pulse and the scent of her powder wafted up to him.

The force of the hand monitoring her racing pulse erased all Searle's resolutions to remain unaffected by him. She knew then that she would give in, but still she tried to fight it. Twisting her head away, she looked directly into his eyes. It was her undoing. The naked desire flashing there slashed through her willpower.

"Searle," murmured Buck and she wanted, needed him to kiss her. But his lips only lightly brushed the silk of her hair. "Seven?" he prodded, his voice low, almost harsh.

"That's early for me," she said, sighing. "Let's make it seven-thirty."

She was rewarded with the sunniest display of gleaming teeth she'd ever seen. He looked, she thought, like a small boy on Christmas day. It seemed he would continually be keeping her off-balance, looking so boyish one minute and so overpoweringly all-male the next.

It was the all-male Buck who flashed a wolfish grin as he released her to stroll to the door. "And, Searle, if you want to eat dinner," he advised over his shoulder, "wear something less revealing than your current attire—or be prepared to *be* dinner!"

Once again, he'd left her on a taunting note. *He must have more lines than a deep-sea fisherman,* thought Searle as she bolted the lock on her door. But she couldn't deny that he was amusing in an earthy way. Nor could she deny his magnetic effect on her senses; it took her some time to calm the rapid thumping of her heart enough to sleep.

Following a staff meeting the next morning that effectively eliminated all thoughts unrelated to the next *Our Town* deadline, Searle barricaded herself behind a pile of papers spread across her desk and threw herself into her work. Lenn used the weekly midweek conferences to keep tabs on every aspect of the magazine's production, from content to layout, and he would as readily bully as cajole to get what he wanted when he wanted it, from his staff. Today, he'd tossed an unexpected interview at Searle, cavalierly ignoring her already full schedule. The interview, with a local woman who had sold her first romantic novel, would probably take up most of her afternoon, which meant Searle had to get twice as much done this morning.

Immersed as she was, she didn't bother to look up from her typewriter when a rapid knock was followed by the opening of her door.

"Can you make it later, Norm?" she asked. "I really have a backlog of work and Lenn's cracking the whip today."

"Norm will definitely have to make it later, but I can't,"

came the breezy reply that instantly tore through her ability to function.

With measured movements, she turned off her machine and swiveled to face him. He was looking at her with that look, the one that so openly hungered for her it made her weak.

"What are you doing here?" she inquired without the least vestige of enthusiasm.

"You know, I'm going to have to send you to one of those places that teaches you how to greet people without sounding as if you wish they weren't there," commented Buck easily. He came forward, closing her door and leaning against the olive metal of her file cabinet. The wild array of flowers had brought a flash of a grin before he returned his dark eyes to devour her.

"I do greet people that way—when I wish they were here," she said dryly.

Buck's casual masculinity overshadowed everything else in her small office. His hands were stuffed into his jeans, emphasizing both the breadth of his shoulders and the narrower line of his hips, an effect further heightened by the tight fit of his yellow T-shirt. Searle forced herself to look away, reminding herself that she should resist his charms, but the elated excitement of being with him surged forth, unbidden, unwanted.

"I hope you're not saying you don't wish me here, Searle," he chided mildly. "My ego's just about down for the count with you anyway." His air of supreme confidence told her quite otherwise; she arched her brows to show her disbelief.

"The point is," she said coolly, "that I have work to do. What are you doing here?"

He left his post by the cabinet to lean over her desk. "I couldn't wait until tomorrow night, after all. So I thought I'd take you to lunch."

Distinctly aware of each movement he made, Searle

tried to still the disquieting rush of her heightened senses. She maintained a dismissive tone when she spoke.

"I wasn't planning on taking lunch today. I've far too much to catch up on here."

"Don't tell me you're on a diet," he said on a note of reproach. He ran an appraising eye over her khaki dress, nodding at the rainbow cinch-belt about her slim waist. "As I said before, you're slender enough. You need to eat more, not less, as far as I'm concerned."

"Your concerns do not concern me," she returned, trying vainly to put a chill into her voice. "As I said, it's a matter of work."

"So where do you want to go eat?" he asked, precisely as if she had not spoken.

Far too conscious of the bare muscular arms propping the broad frame of him against her desktop, Searle pushed one pile of papers atop another, refusing to look at him. The sheer sensuality of his presence both irritated and intrigued her. Nervously ruffling another stack of papers, she asked, "Do you always take control of people like this?"

"Oh, no," he denied. She heard his laugh and raised her head. The sable eyes told her he was enjoying her discomfort. "Only people who need control. Like you. Come to lunch with me, Searle."

"I suppose," she said frostily, "that it's the only way to get rid of you."

She stood and he straightened. She'd known she would go from the moment she'd seen him. What annoyed her was she saw that Carlton had known it, too. Someone, she thought as they walked down the hall together, someone ought to take this guy down a peg or two. She ignored the stares they generated; with a sigh, she accepted the fact that speculation would spread through the building faster than a fire over prairie grass.

Outside, Searle paused, but Buck strode off purposefully, so she followed him wordlessly. Sun glinted over his blond hair and, as she glanced sideways at him, she knew a momentary, foolish wish to touch the thick gold of it. He stopped beside her car, weight on one foot and palm out.

"Where's your car?" she asked icily, digging through her purse.

"Still in the shop." He took the keys from her, smiled widely, and added, "A buddy of mine dropped me off here."

"And just how," she queried, knowing the answer, "do you intend to get home?"

"I was hoping you'd offer to drop me off at the stadium after lunch."

"You hoped wrong," she stated emphatically. "I've already told you, I'm buried in work."

"Work's not everything, Searle," he pointed out, watching her closely as she buckled her seat belt. "Besides," he tacked on with his rumbling laugh, "I *am* work, remember? Where to, lady?"

He ignored the glare this earned him and the haughty tone with which Searle directed him to the nearby Mexican restaurant, but talked easily about the tune-up on his car. "I'll have it back by tomorrow night, don't worry."

"Oh, believe me," she said with heavy sarcasm, "I don't worry about tomorrow night at all. I don't even think about it."

Searle was relieved when they pulled into the restaurant's parking lot. Even the briefest ride with him so close tensed her every muscle. She wondered if every woman felt this upheaval when near him, then immediately mocked her stupidity. Of course they did. Who could not feel weak with desire when confronted with his potent sexuality? Especially when his eyes narrowed with unhidden passion, as they did now?

Buck came around to open the door for her, and Searle

attempted to ignore his outstretched hand, brushing past him. He simply encircled the flesh of her arm instead, delighting in the slight quiver Searle could not suppress.

They did not speak again until they had been seated, served drinks, and left to study the menus. Then, letting his beer stand, Buck eyed her with such fixed intensity that at last Searle dropped her menu to demand, "Just what is wrong? Have my eyes crossed or something?"

"It's your hair," he explained.

"My hair?" she repeated blankly.

"You shouldn't wear it rolled up like that," he scolded. "You shouldn't deny everyone the beauty of it. When I think of the way it cascaded over your shoulders last night—"

"I do not wish to discuss my hair!" she snapped, looking quickly about to see if any of her co-workers were present to overhear and possibly misconstrue his words.

"What do you wish to discuss?" he inquired with interest.

"Nothing!"

Mercifully, the waitress appeared to save Searle from whatever Buck had been about to say. When she ordered a salad, she didn't see his brows draw together. The young waitress shook with excitement as she turned to Buck.

"Could I—could I have your autograph?" she asked timidly. The look of adoration she focused on him made Searle cross. No doubt about it, women toppled like pins in a bowling alley over him.

"Sure thing," said Buck, taking the girl's pen and scribbling over a napkin. As he handed it to her, he grinned and said, "I'll have the enchilada plate, and please bring the lady a burrito to go along with her salad."

"But I don't want a burrito," protested Searle, stopping the waitress from taking the order.

"She'll have the burrito," said Buck with quiet determination. "Unless you'd prefer a taco?" he added with a glance toward Searle.

She said nothing and Buck again told the waitress to get a burrito. The young girl wrote it down with a questioning look at Searle, then quirked her lips nervously and left.

"I won't eat it," declared Searle with a hiss as soon as they were alone.

"You will," returned Buck complacently. He sipped his beer, then said with a coaxing smile, "You need a good meal if you're to get through all that work you've got to do."

"I'm not hungry," she said stubbornly. "You've no right to order food for me."

"Don't you know the body's a vessel and all that?" he asked.

His eyes were twinkling. She realized that he was amused. It annoyed her to realize she always seemed to amuse him. Even in his most passionate moments, she remembered. *Damn him,* she thought.

"And with *such* a vessel," continued Buck, ignoring the frown she focused on him, "you must take better care of yourself. Believe me, it's the best damn vessel I've ever seen."

Pressing her lips against the cool rim of her glass, Searle took a sip of margarita and calculated her response. This guy seemed to know instinctively what to say, what to do to throw her off-balance every time, but she was catching on. Having taught herself over the years how not to fall into a man's clutches, she'd thought she knew every trick in the book, and perhaps she did. But it was apparent that with Carlton, it was going to take the kind of effort she hadn't put forth since her adolescent years.

"Don't think I don't know what you're doing," she remarked as she set down the glass and licked the moisture from her lips.

"Oh? What am I doing?" he returned, brown eyes fixed steadily on the movement of her tongue.

"You think you'll roll me over with that massive manly charm of yours," she answered, very coolly. "But I warn you, I'm made of sterner stuff."

"Thanks for the warning, but I doubt I needed it." He grinned lopsidedly and Searle turned her eyes to the crystals of salt studding the rim of her glass. Better not to look at that grin, she thought.

This jock had a way of growing on you. The confident smile, the ready charm, had a surprising foundation of intelligence. She had to admit that she might even like him, if he weren't so dangerous. But Buck Carlton was definitely dangerous as far as she was concerned. He had an uncanny ability to reach out and touch the woman few suspected existed under the sophisticated reserve, and that made him number one on her most-dangerous list.

Eyeing her over the edge of his frosted mug, Buck took a sip of his beer, then set his glass down. Suddenly, he asked, "Has there ever been anyone, Searle?"

She looked at him then, puzzlement in her eyes. "Anyone?" she repeated.

"You know, a steady guy," he explained briefly. "Surely a woman as lovely as you has had someone in her life. I can't believe some guy hasn't snapped you up."

Her green eyes mirrored the frost on his mug, her tone echoed the chips of ice floating in her margarita. "Some women have higher ambitions in life than to be 'snapped up.' "

"But you're far too special not to have had someone," he insisted stubbornly. His sable eyes never left her face and he quickly noted the threads of color crossing her prominent cheekbones.

"My private life is just that—private," she returned bitingly.

The appearance of the young waitress with their two

plates put an end to the potentially hostile discussion. Searle began to eat the burrito without protest, grateful to have something to occupy her.

After a few tense moments, Buck began to chat easily about himself and his background, and he continued to do so throughout lunch, calming the atmosphere between them.

"I had a great childhood," he told her. "Oregon's a great place to grow up. I had the Rogue River and the Cascade Mountains to play in, and my folks encouraged me to take advantage of the outdoors—rafting, hiking, skiing. Do you ski, Searle?"

"No," she answered with a relaxed smile. She couldn't help it; he had somehow managed to make her feel content to be with him, listening to his life story.

"Then I'll teach you this winter," he said. She forbore telling him he wouldn't be teaching her anything and he went blithely on. "You'll love my folks. They're still as active as ever. And as happy, even after thirty-three years of marriage. They're the reason I know you were wrong the other night. People like my parents prove that marriage can work."

She sat upright, looking at him coldly. She didn't want to discuss his parents' marriage, or any other. He watched her, a quizzical line crossing his brow.

"You don't believe that, do you?" he asked after a long pause. "But just wait 'til you meet them—"

"I doubt," she interrupted dampingly, "that I'll be meeting your parents. Shall we go?"

He downed the end of his beer and paid, not pressing the point. He'd seen her stiffen at the first mention of marriage and was wondering what the hell had offended her. He was still wondering when, several minutes later, they were on the freeway heading toward the southeast location of Blues' Stadium.

"Why did you do that?" he suddenly inquired, bursting

into the stream of thought that Searle had been using in an attempt to ignore his presence.

"Do what?" she asked, bewildered.

"Stiffen when I told you about my parents."

She stiffened now, she couldn't help it. Observing her from the corner of his eye, Buck saw it and immediately demanded, "Now what the hell is wrong?"

"Nothing. Nothing is wrong," she denied, her voice losing all semblance of warmth.

"Don't give me that bull," returned Buck. "You've got more defenses than the Pentagon, but if you think you can put me off, you're in for a shock."

She didn't respond. She turned her head away to stare unseeing out the window. *He will not get through, he will not,* she told herself, as if the telling would make it so. She wouldn't let him set the trap for her.

With a side glance at her averted profile, he stated reasonably, "I know you don't believe in the institution, but surely you don't condemn every marriage. Some people do make it work, you know."

"Of course I don't," she instantly asserted, although in fact, she did. "But you needn't constantly bring the subject up." She sounded childishly petulant and she knew it. When he said nothing more, she sat silent, peeved that she'd again let him rattle her.

As they pulled into the ball-park lot and stopped, Buck turned to face her, his arm stretched over the top of the steering wheel.

"You might as well save that get-lost look for someone else. It doesn't work on me. Are you coming to tonight's game?"

He sounded abrupt, almost harsh. She figured it was the blow to his ego that made him hostile, the fact that she didn't crumple onto his broad shoulder and bare her soul —not to mention the rest of her—to him.

"Well, are you?" he goaded.

"No," she replied blandly.

"Suit yourself," he said, unfolding himself from her car at last. "See you tomorrow night. And, Searle," he added as he dangled her keys above her palm.

"Yes?" she said on a snap.

"Don't keep trying to make me angry. You wouldn't really like it if you succeeded." He dropped the keys into her hand and stalked away, leaving her wondering what on earth he meant.

She drove out of the lot with an angry little squeal of rubber against concrete.

CHAPTER SIX

Romance was the last topic Searle wanted to delve into that afternoon, but somehow she managed to approach her interview with her usual professional gloss. She kept her attention focused on the local writer, relentlessly ignoring the part of her mind that continually drifted toward visions of tanned muscles rippling with power as they leapt and stretched and flexed. With careful questioning, she manipulated the interview, extracting good quotes and colorful information. This was how an interview should be conducted, she thought with satisfaction; satisfaction that dimmed as it invited unwelcome comparisons with her last, disastrous interview.

When Chris Rinchisen, the Midwest photographer, took over, snapping shot after shot of the novelist at her desk, images of Buck pervaded Searle's mind. Outwardly serene, she watched Chris in action and asked herself why she let Carlton get to her. It would be a mistake to get involved with him. She didn't want to get involved with anyone. Involvement meant allowing someone to see what no one else saw and that meant being made vulnerable. She had no intention of opening herself up, especially not to Buck Carlton. That was a relationship clearly doomed from the start. After tomorrow night, she would write up her story and that would be the end of it.

The next day, routine provided the balm for her inner misgivings about her date. Arguing with Lenn over a bit of blue-penciling he'd done on one of her pieces released some of her escalating jitters, but as morning crawled into afternoon Searle's ability to concentrate on her work evaporated. The suburban papers came out on Wednesdays and half the editorial staff seemed to disappear on

Thursdays. The resulting quiet emphasized the clamor of her nerves and eventually she knew there was really only one cure for her. Glaring accusingly at the bright bouquet crowning her file cabinet, Searle cleared her desk, covered her typewriter, collected her purse, and left. It was midafternoon.

Some perverse vanity in her wanted to knock Carlton flat, and her preparations over the next several hours rivaled those of an Olympic contender gearing up for the games. The results, from the luster of her carefully tousled raven tresses to the glitter of her silver-tinted nails, were breathtaking. Hoping Buck's idea of a good time did not consist solely of a pizza parlor and beer, Searle had dressed with a slick elegance. A straight black sheath with spaghetti straps intensified the sleek lines of her alluring figure and a sheer, silvery jacket added an intriguing element of sparkle. As she added the final touch of a single diamond-on-platinum pendant, the harsh chime of her doorbell caused her to miss the clasp and drop the necklace. Scooping the jewel from the carpet, she went in answer to the second impatient ring.

Searle was accustomed to receiving gifts from men, usually roses, small pieces of jewelry, occasionally even candy. But she was not accustomed to Buck Carlton and certainly not prepared for the sight that greeted her when she opened the door.

A giant stuffed mouse provocatively wiggled its enormous ears, then flopped into her astonished arms.

"You need a pet," explained Buck blandly as he followed the mouse into her apartment.

She nuzzled the softness of the pink and white fur a moment before peeping up at him over the tip of one gigantic ear. Instantly, she was grateful for the stuffed toy, which hid her face, for she knew her mouth gaped open. He was wearing a conservative dove-gray suit that fit over his form so well it could only have been custom-made, while a shirt with the merest tint of blue provided a showcase for a dark navy tie striped with thin gray streaks. The casual disorder of the sun-bleached blond hair and the uplifting of the sandy moustache told her, however, that it was indeed Buck standing there grinning at her.

The grin gradually faded as the silence stretched between them. "Well, if you don't like him," he said at last, "we can always put him up for adoption."

"Oh, no. He's mine," said Searle quickly and, to her secret surprise, meaning it. "I'll keep him—even though we're not allowed pets in these apartments."

As she spoke, she set the mouse onto the corner of her sofa. She turned to find Buck regarding her with that devouring look that never failed to make her legs feel like liquid.

"You're very prompt," she commented politely to cover her confusion. "I just have to add this necklace and I'll be ready." She dangled the pendant.

"You certainly don't need any jewels to add to your beauty," said Buck quietly. "You're a knockout in that dress."

She had meant to impress him and she had succeeded, but somehow Searle felt as if she were the one who'd just been flattened. Her nerves seemed to leap and dive like a roller coaster as he continued to let his darkening eyes survey her inch by inch. Before she could react, he took the necklace from her quivering fingers, then spun her around.

As Buck's arms came around her, draping the pendant against the creamy smoothness of her skin, Searle stiffened. His fingers feathered the back of her neck as he fiddled with the clasp, causing an electric shiver to speed down her spine. Within moments, Buck had fastened the tiny hinge and moved away, but his tingling effect upon her lingered.

Remaining impassively cordial, Searle thanked him,

picked up her small silver clutch bag and pronounced herself ready. Outside, Buck led her to a metallic-blue BMW, and the realization that this jock had class caused a severe readjustment in her thinking. To cover her disquiet, she began a light discussion about christening her new "pet." After several suggestions, which she promptly rejected, she demanded time to think and fell into a reverie.

Turning off the freeway, they drove down wide, tree-lined boulevards embellished with fountained median strips, a mark of the city. The late-evening summer sun splayed warm rays through the trees, checkering the streets and teasing over them as they passed swiftly by. The view, however, did not hold Searle's attention. Running her fingers along the edge of her silvery jacket, she concentrated on resisting the lure of Buck's masculine magnetism.

Stealing a glance at his profile, she noted the strength in the cut of his squared jawline. The powerful capability defined by that jaw attracted Searle in a way that went far beyond her appreciation of his glowingly all-American good looks. Hidden behind the thick fringe of her lowered lashes, her eyes traveled slowly downward, past the solid outline of his chest to the firm width of his thighs. With an inner flush, she quickly looked back out the windshield. Just the brief sight of those toned muscles caused her heart to miss a beat and Searle experienced a wave of longing that astonished her.

She didn't *want* to want him! Wanting a man like Buck would make her a prime candidate for the men in little white coats. She and Buck would mix about as well as oil and water. Her sudden flare of physical desire for him would have been laughable if it weren't so dangerous. But she knew the first glow of desire would quickly fade to leave pain and anger, disappointment and heartache. Wanting a ladies' man like Buck would be about as sensible as lighting a match in a dynamite factory.

Her attention was wrenched back to her surroundings when Buck slowed, turning into a curving drive. Surprise and pleasure swept over her in equal parts as she recognized the elegant edifice of the Grand Restaurant. A doorman sprang to open her door, then Buck was at her side, collecting her elbow and steering her toward the entrance.

"Well?" asked Buck as they mounted the steps together.

"I'm very pleased," she said sincerely. "I love to eat here and on my budget that's a rare occurrence."

"I meant, did you come up with a name?" he explained, his sable eyes glittering with laughter.

"Not yet," she confessed, refusing to meet his look. In the jumble of her thoughts, she had completely forgotten about the mouse, but she couldn't tell him that.

They were met at the door by a short, stout man in tails who led them silently to a corner table. Entering the Grand always made Searle feel as if she were entering an older, more peaceful world. As she sank into the luxury of the red velvet seat that the maître d' held out for her, Searle admired the view of one of the city's finest parks through the leaded windows. It was quite simply one of the best tables in the restaurant and she smiled her appreciation at her escort, who acknowledged it with an audacious wink.

As the diminutive headwaiter vanished, Buck leaned across the crisp white linen tablecloth and cupped her hand within his. In the subdued light of the flickering candles, his dark eyes glimmered like the cut crystal at his elbow. "Happy?" he asked softly.

From deep in the center of the vast room came the faint strains of a violin sonata; Searle could just see the outline of the musician as he milked the beauty from his instrument. Casting a look over the dignified grandeur of the room, she brought her eyes to meet Buck's over the flame of the candle.

"Yes," she said simply. Then, buffering her remark with

a disarming smile, she added casually, "I certainly didn't picture you as the sort of man at home in this type of restaurant."

"Well, I have to admit I'm more at home at a hot dog stand," he responded easily. "But I try to enjoy all types of experiences."

"I rather feared you might have a hot dog stand in mind for tonight," admitted Searle in a throaty, teasing tone that darkened the glow in Buck's eyes.

"No way. I could see at a glance you weren't that kind of lady. 'This woman has Class with a capital C,' I said to myself the moment I saw you."

Searle regarded their entwined hands for a long moment. He was gently rubbing his thumb over the top of her hand, but he stopped the motion as she stared. Then she withdrew her hand to her lap. "Yes, I've heard that you have a vast experience of women's tastes," she said expressionlessly.

His thick brows drew together, but the sudden appearance of the sommelier cut off the comment hovering on his lips. As he discussed the wine selection with the waiter, Buck displayed a knowledge that Searle recognized as superior. When he chose a sweet Italian aperitif and a spectacular dry Bordeaux for dinner, she had to admit she was impressed.

The wine soon eased the undercurrent of tension between them, and long before their chateaubriand was delivered by a nearly invisible waiter, they were conversing with the casual affability of old friends. For the most part, conversation over the leisurely dinner remained impersonal, ranging from a surprising mutual enjoyment of Charles Dickens to sharp disagreement on the merits of rock and roll. At one point, Buck leaned forward, the iridescent glimmer of the candlelight reflecting in the depths of his chocolate eyes.

"I'm beginning to understand why poets write about love at first sight," he said in a voice oddly husky.

All expression disappeared from Searle's face, leaving it masked in coldness. A flash of anger briefly flared within her. Why was he spoiling the evening this way? Her lashes fell against her cheeks, shuttering her eyes. "Are you?" she returned in a voice guaranteed to freeze.

"Do you believe in love?" he parried, watching her closely.

"I believe," she stated firmly, "that this conversation is unnecessary." She glanced up at him through her lowered lashes, then quickly looked away. His intent, direct gaze had a curious effect on her nerves, leaving her breathless and jittery, as if he had touched her.

"Why?" prodded Buck. "Does that mean love is on your list of taboos, like marriage?"

Taking control of herself, Searle forced herself to meet his steady look. "What it means, Buck, is that my personal beliefs, likes, or habits are none of your business. Let's get this straight between us—I am not going to be your conquest of the month."

He laughed, but the line of his jaw went taut and the glint in his eyes sharpened. Unable to withstand the cut of his gaze, Searle dropped her eyes to where her jacket dusted the ivory cloth of the table. The light caught the silver sparkle of her sleeve, holding it a moment before dancing away. Buck introduced another subject, and when she again dared to look up, he was leaning negligently in his chair, the razor-edge gleam gone from his eyes.

It wasn't long before Searle relaxed again, pushing out of her mind the disturbing reaction of her senses to his earlier comments. By the time the tall silver pot of coffee arrived, she was laughing easily over anecdotes of his days as a rookie with the team. Continual pranks and practical jokes relieved boredom and frayed nerves, he told her, especially when the team was on the road.

She took a leisurely sip of her coffee, then stared into her porcelain cup before remarking, "The sport certainly perpetuates boyhood."

Her eyes remained fixed on the depths of her coffee and she did not see the frown come into Buck's eyes. Bringing the cup to her lips, she added with a careful change of tone, "What did you do with your day off?"

The cloud slowly passed from his eyes and he answered smoothly, "I spent the major portion of the day standing in a shower, grinning my fool head off. At least it left me squeaky clean for tonight." Responding to the puzzlement in her slanting green eyes, he went on to explain, "I was filming a commercial for So-Clean soap. I couldn't fit in the time to fly to California, so they brought in a film crew and in just five hours of scrubbing, I was 'Oh-So-Clean.' "

"Norman told me you were doing national commercials now," she remarked thoughtfully.

"So who's Norman?" questioned Buck sharply.

"He's an advertising executive at Midwest."

Since her tone was noncommittal, this did not tell Buck what he wanted to know. He asked, "Is he a—friend?"

The brief hesitation made his meaning clear. She lifted a brow disdainfully and replied with a touch of icy hauteur. "I suppose you could call him that."

"Dammit, Searle, stop playing word games with me," muttered Buck. "You know damn well what I mean."

"I've gone out with Norm a couple of times," she said in the same haughty tone. "Not that it's any of your business."

He surprised her by letting that pass, shifting mood with the alacrity that kept Searle spinning. The smile that generally hovered beneath the thick moustache reappeared as he began to describe in vivid detail the trials and tribulations of filming a thirty-second television commercial. All the while, Searle was intensely aware of him, of the way he tilted his head back to laugh, trapping the gilt of the candlelight in his golden hair; of the way he occasionally stroked the thickness of his moustache, drawing her attention to his square, sensual lips; of the way he half closed his eyes with unexpected emotion as he looked at her. Though she tried to resist it, each action aroused her senses in a way that maddened her. Suddenly, she realized he'd asked her something.

"I beg your pardon?" she said. "I didn't hear that."

"I should be offended," he said with a teasing smile, "but I'm getting used to your blows to my ego. It's a good thing it's such a tough little fellow. I asked you, my darling, inattentive Searle, if you'd like to see the view of Stillwater Lake as seen from my deck. It's pretty spectacular, especially at night."

She didn't answer for a moment, her mind still ringing with the huskiness of his voice as he said "my darling," but the sudden frown in his eyes brought a response at last. Somehow keeping her voice level, she said politely, "I suppose so. If that's what you would like."

He stared at her for a second, then the lids dropped over his eyes. He'd been leaning rather casually into his chair, but he now sat forward. "I think I will get offended," he snapped. "Is that all the enthusiasm you can work up? Or is enthusiasm one of the things you don't allow yourself? Like enjoyment?"

Taken aback, Searle had no reply. She sat staring at him, only the widening of her slanted eyes indicating her astonishment over his flare of temper. Watching her, Buck stifled an urge to shake her until her teeth rattled. In the few days of their acquaintance, she had managed to stretch his temper to limits few had ever reached and he found himself wondering just when the elastic would finally snap. She continued to say nothing and suddenly he shrugged, then smiled ruefully.

"You, Searle Delacorte," he stated with emphasis, "are playing hell with my emotional equilibrium."

He abruptly signaled for the waiter, who materialized immediately. While he signed the check, Searle studied him from beneath lowered lashes. She understood his feelings. No matter how much she struggled against it, he was churning up her own long-hidden feelings, shaking her firm belief that hers was the only possible choice in life. The novelty of her emotional confusion affected her like an amusement park ride, thrilling her one moment and horrifying her the next. When he stood, she rose gracefully to her feet and cast another surreptitious glance at his face.

If she expected him to remain put out with her, Searle didn't know Buck. His bad temper was mercurial; he preferred to enjoy life cheerfully, not rage at it. As his BMW was brought forward, he began explaining how he came to build his house on Stillwater Lake. He made no other reference to being offended and gradually Searle joined the conversation. As he drove with controlled speed onto the freeway, they lapsed into a silence that she could only describe as companionable.

CHAPTER SEVEN

The full moon hung like a haloed dot in a Van Gogh painting. Staring into the infinity of the dark canvas of the sky, Searle let her mind pleasantly drift. Whatever she had expected of an evening out with Buck, it hadn't been this. Impressed with his command at the restaurant, beguiled by his amusing and interesting conversation, she had to admit she'd enjoyed his company. Despite all her resolutions to remain impervious to his earthy charm, she had responded warmly to him. He had been every bit as personable as he was attractive. And he was so damned attractive.

Repressing that dangerous line of thinking, she felt a sudden need to break the tranquillity that somehow seemed to bind her to him. Without moving her eyes from the night scenes out the window, she asked quietly, "How long did you say you'd lived out by the Lake?"

"I didn't say," he answered in a voice that seemed to caress her, "but it's been about two years. We're nearly there," he added, briefly treating himself to a glance at her patrician profile.

Even as he spoke, he slowed the car for a sharp bend leading away from the two-lane highway they'd been on. As tall shadowed trees blocked the inky sky from view, Searle studied the clasp on her clutch. She tried vainly to remember the last time she had let a man take her to his place. *Why,* she demanded of herself, *did I ever agree to this?* She didn't want to get any further involved with this jock—with any man. It must have been the Bordeaux. Whatever it was, she decided to end the evening as quickly as possible. One brief tour of his house and then home, she promised herself firmly as Buck turned onto a paved drive and stopped.

"Well, this is it. Want to see my etchings, little girl?" he inquired with a playful leer that confirmed her suspicions as to what he had on *his* mind.

He got out, then walked around to open her door and give her a hand as she got smoothly out. Through the trees, she glimpsed the shimmer of water, heard the hushed rustle of wind before Buck whisked her through the door of his rough wood house and directly into an expansive, high-ceilinged room that was both well-furnished and comfortable.

Crossing the thick cement-gray carpet, Buck loosened the knot of his tie. As he thrust open a paneled half-door, revealing a well-stocked bar, he tossed the tie casually onto its ledge. He shrugged out of his jacket and discarded it beside the tie. Searle eyed both items with disfavor. She felt like the fly to Buck's spider as she stepped slowly into his web.

"Drink?" he asked, splashing an amber liquid into a glass.

"No, thank you," she said stiffly as she glanced about the room. It was nothing like she had expected. Dominated by wood beams and floor-to-ceiling windows, everything about it came tastefully together. She perched gingerly on the edge of a brick-red leather chair that offset the deep brown sofa and naturally drew one's eye to the brick fireplace. Glass in hand, Buck lounged over to take possession of the matching chair opposite her.

"Like it?" he inquired casually over the rim of his glass.

"It's very nice." She cast another admiring look about the room, pausing at the one wall, which provided a backdrop for video and stereo equipment so sophisticated it made her blink. Her eye was drawn back to Buck by the movement of his hand as he set his glass down on a low, wooden table covered with a number of magazines. "Yes," she repeated, "it's very nice."

"Like to see the rest of the place?" he asked, standing with one hand extended toward her.

She ignored the hand, rising fluidly. "Certainly." The sooner she saw it all, the sooner she would be out the door, free of his disturbing presence. With her heart beating erratically beneath the black sheath gown, she allowed Buck to take her hand after all and lead her through his home. Well, she hadn't precisely allowed him to; he'd taken it with the air of a man who has a perfect right to her hand and she had meekly acquiesced. *Definitely too much Bordeaux,* she thought.

After quick glimpses of an enormous, cheerfully sparkling kitchen, a rather formal dining room, two guest rooms, and one standard bathroom, he escorted her into a giant cavern of a room.

"This is where the etchings are supposed to be," he said with a sly wink.

Her eyes slid over the rumpled indigo spread of a king-sized waterbed, then resolutely moved elsewhere. The masculine intimacy of it disturbed her in an elemental way she did not want to define. Glancing past the unlit gray-stone fireplace, she saw Buck eyeing her with a knowing look that proclaimed his amusement.

"Cozy," she said with just the right inflection of cynicism.

"I think so," he agreed. "But wait 'til you see this." He walked to a pair of oak doors on the far side of the room and, flinging them open, gestured to her. As she neared, she raised her arched brows.

"Just what every modern home cannot do without," she remarked dryly.

A sunken marble bath, complete with gilt fixtures shaped like seashells, loomed before her. One mirrored wall caught the gleam of the gilt and threw it back at them.

"Care to try it?" offered Buck, his grin tilting up his moustache. "It'll seat two very comfortably."

"I'm sure you would know," replied Searle in her coolest voice. "No, thank you, I think I'd like to complete the tour."

"What you need," he said as he shut the double doors, "is a more adventurous spirit."

"Oh? I'd thought it was more color in my life that I needed."

"That, too. Actually, what I really think you need is me," said Buck with the merest hint of mockery. "But then, I've always believed I'm just what every woman needs."

Gazing up into the teasing laughter in his creased eyes, Searle's breath quickened. She knew she should play along with the joke, but the sudden pounding of her pulses drummed out her ability to do so. Instead, she responded in a subzero voice, "I am quite certain you have. Has every woman thought so, too?" she queried, then could have kicked herself for doing so.

Leaning back against the door frame, Buck ran a paw of a hand negligently through the sun-streaked richness of his thick hair. "Well, up to now I've been pretty irresistible. But recently I seemed to have developed this incredible resistibility—perhaps you'd care to help me regain my fading masculine confidence?" he suggested with a lopsided grin.

The grin had its effect. A smile parted her deep-red lips and a lightness returned to her tone. "Oh, believe me, Buck Carlton, you don't need one iota more of confidence." She shook her head, feathering her shoulders with the clouds of her ebony hair.

It was with an effort that Buck straightened. "Come on, I'll show you downstairs," he said, an unfathomable harshness underscoring his words.

Searle looked at him quizzically as she followed him

away from his bedroom. He made no attempt to recapture her hand and she was annoyed to realize that this disappointed her.

One half of the basement contained yet another fireplace and a wet bar. The other half had been converted into an exercise room with weights, pulleys, and other complicated-looking equipment positioned throughout. At the end of the long tiled floor an archway gave a view of a Jacuzzi. Searle caught sight of a slick black one-piece suit draped over a lone chair by the Jacuzzi and wondered cynically if it belonged to Buck's "close friend," the florist. Not that she gave a damn, of course.

"Would you like to go for a moonlight swim? I've got a suit that fits all sizes," he added.

She looked again at the slick swimsuit and felt a rising swell of anger. It was obviously his standard line and she wasn't about to fall for it. Keeping her voice coldly remote, she declined. "I think not. It is a work night for me and I can't stay too long."

His sandy brows elevated, a bare frown sketched between them. He hated that arctic tone of hers and in a chilling attempt to match it, he said, "Fine. Let's go back up."

They returned to the living room without speaking, Buck following behind her on the stairs. She could feel the glancing touch of his arm against the back of her thigh as they climbed, and her heart hammered in fierce acknowledgment of the feather touch. She told herself to quit being ridiculous. It was only his arm, for God's sake! But the relief she felt as they emerged from the narrow stairway was unmistakable.

He surprised her by lightly taking her elbow and steering her through his living room to a panel of rust-colored curtains. Drawing these wide, he revealed a wall of glass.

"I promised you a view from my deck, didn't I?" he said as he slid open one pane.

As they stepped out onto an expanse of redwood, the night breeze caressed her warm skin and stirred the ends of her hair. Buck leaned against the wood railing and stared out into the distance. Standing close enough to feel the warmth of his body, but without touching him, Searle looked out over the railing's edge. Stillwater Lake had been aptly named, she thought, gazing at the glassy sheet of water resplendent with the brilliant reflection of the moon's golden threads. Soft rustles sounded around her. She felt, rather than saw, him draw closer.

"How do you like it?" he asked, his voice softly hesitant, as if her answer mattered a great deal.

Though she did not look directly at him, Searle was aware of the way the wind ruffled the gilt of his hair, of the way his breath had deepened, adding to the susurrus of the night.

"It's as spectacular as you claimed," she replied in a contralto made huskier by stirrings she could not deny.

"And the house? Did you like that?" he pursued, moving nearer still, until the hard contours of his body were touching the softness of her curves.

She turned, determined to step away from him. The breeze caught the edge of her sheer silvery jacket and lifted it away as one thin strap of her gown slid down her shoulder. She saw Buck's eyes glitter strangely as they followed the motion of the strap. Then his heavy lids dropped over his eyes and his arms wrapped around her. Knowing she should, Searle did not resist as he pulled her into the mold of his frame. His hands twined into her hair. She felt his breath graze her cheek.

"I've waited all night to do this," he murmured hoarsely. "God, how I want you."

"Please, don't," she protested weakly. A sensation of desire was stealing over her, robbing her of her power to withstand him.

"Please, don't," he mocked gently. Not releasing her,

continuing to explore her cheek with the light touch of his lips, he taunted, "Why not let me touch you? Afraid you might respond? That you might actually feel something beneath all the icy reserve?"

Before she could react, Buck's mouth captured the fullness of hers and she shuddered with a pleasure that would not be stilled.

"I won't hurt you, Searle," he breathed raggedly against her lips before intensifying his kiss.

As his lips burrowed forcefully into hers, demanding a response, his hands slowly began to trace the outlines of her body. Methodically, they moved from the nape of her neck to the swell of her breasts, downward to the curve of her hips, sending a trembling through her that increased in fervor as his fingers reached the base of her spine, and her lips parted under his.

Reluctantly withdrawing from the inflamed fullness of her mouth, Buck laced kisses into the silk of her hair, then whispered thickly, "You enjoy it when I do this, don't you?"

"No—yes—I don't know," she answered in muffled confusion. He was forcing her to respond in ways she'd never dreamed possible and, for the moment, she gave herself up to the heady excitement of his every kiss.

"Touch me, Searle," he commanded, his voice a soft surration. "Touch me."

Unhurried, in a world without time or sense, Searle's hands delicately brushed the breadth of his chest. His quiver of pleasure, his keen gasp for breath at her brief touch, filled her with a feminine power. Her fingers teased with light flicks as she slowly loosened each button of his shirt. Slipping her hands beneath the thin fabric, she splayed her fingers over his heated flesh. His chest was smooth, only lightly tufted with hair, so that she felt the full impact of his muscles tensing, his heartbeat quickening wildly. With gentle deliberation, she began to knead the firm muscles, glorying when Buck groaned against her lips in response.

Abruptly, with the flat of one hand, he pressed her closer against his hardened thighs as his other hand tantalizingly retraced its way up to the soft curve of her breast, cupping it, tenderly caressing it. As his fingers seared her through the flimsy barrier of her sheath, she heard a whispered moan, then dimly realized it came from her own lips. The realization brought with it a sudden, overwhelming fear of herself, of her unrestrained response.

What was she doing? Did she want to become another of Buck Carlton's prizes, like the showgirl, the model? She had to stop this madness. She had to stamp out the flame of passion that was threatening to engulf her. Forcing herself to smother the desire throbbing within her, Searle stiffened and stood rigidly within his arms, willing herself to cease responding.

Gradually, Buck's hands and lips halted their sensual strokings, and he released her with a growling sigh. For what seemed an eternity, they said nothing, standing motionlessly, staring at each other, breathing in harsh gasps. The glaze of passion receded from Buck's dark eyes. He shrugged. His mouth turned down in frustration, and he began to rebutton his shirt, his eyes raking her form with a look—of what? Contempt?

"All right, Searle," he said finally, his voice soft, as one speaking to a frightened child. "I can be patient. But," he added, grimly straightening his lips, "I wish to heaven I could get my hands on him."

"On who?" she asked, then wondered if that breathless rasp could possibly have been her own voice.

"The bastard who so effectively soured you on feeling anything," he replied tonelessly, his eyes fixed on the rapid rise and fall of her breasts.

Nervously, she readjusted the strap of her gown, noting that his eyes moved to follow her hands. "There wasn't anyone like that," she denied flatly, her voice sounding more normal.

"There must have been," he countered. "You're too damned beautiful to have locked yourself away from your feelings for no reason."

"I have feelings. I feel things!" she objected, strangely upset. Why was he accusing her?

"Yeah—buried under a ton of reserve," he retorted.

"Simply because, unlike you, I approach things logically—"

"Coldly, do you mean?"

Why did she feel a pricking of acute pain at the anger in his voice? She was letting him get to her. It didn't matter to her what he thought of her, so why did she feel this need to explain herself?

"I am not a romanticist, I admit that," she said, her voice slightly unsteady. "But I am mature enough and intelligent enough to know what I want from life, Buck. My 'reserve,' as you call it, is my own choice."

"Whatever you call it, whatever you think justifies it, it all boils down to the fact that you're running scared," stated Buck in a strangely brutal tone. "You're so damned afraid to live—"

"I face up to life!" she cut in, meeting anger with anger.

"But you don't get into life, Searle. There's a big difference between standing at life's edge and being in the center of it."

She stared wordlessly, outraged, for several seconds. Then in a flat, cold voice she said, "If you are quite done psychoanalyzing me, Doctor, I should very much like to be taken home."

"Running away again, Searle?" he taunted. "What is it this time? Me—or your own needs that you can't handle?"

"I don't need to explain my desires or actions to you," she answered with a biting calm. "If you don't wish to drive me, I'll call a cab." Searle turned toward the glass door, intending to put her threat into action.

Buck's hand shot out, roughly shackling her arm. With one emphatic jerk, he yanked her back into his embrace. She stood stiffly, but even as she willed herself to meet his kiss with nothing more than a dutiful politeness, her lips parted in disobedient hunger. Buck's mouth nuzzled into the tousled mass of her black hair, found the tender sensitivity of her earlobe, and finally the smooth skin at the base of her neck. Her body trembled with yearning, quivered with anticipation. She heard him softly groan, a low murmur of need that fueled her own resurgence of desire. Then, as deliberately as he'd taken hold of her, Buck let her go.

"I'll drive you home. Like I said, Searle, I can wait. But I don't intend to be put off. I'm a very persistent guy and I'm going to thaw that frozen shield of yours, Ms. Delacorte. I'm going to find the woman you're so damned afraid to be."

The abrupt tone was matched by a stride that took him from her side, leaving her standing on the deck, shivering in the warm breeze. Somehow, she made her legs move to follow him. *What is happening to me?* she asked over and over, not finding a satisfactory answer. She knew she needed time to think, away from the distraction of her obvious physical need for Buck. The sudden craving for him could be viewed as a natural response to a need too long denied, but she wondered why, oh why, did her body have to select Carlton of all men to yearn for?

She knew he was a man used to getting what he wanted. He would use that bulldozer technique of his to crash right through any barriers she might devise. But what she needed to sort out, what she was reluctant to face, was the undeniable fact that she almost wanted him to tear down those barriers. It was as unthinkable as the idea of a relationship between them.

The short drive between Buck's home and her apartment complex seemed lengthened by the strained silence between them. When he pulled into a parking slot she quickly opened her door and said without expression, "There's no need for you to see me up. Thanks for the lovely dinner."

"Don't be childish," he said mildly as he got out and came around to her side.

She did not respond to the reproach, though inwardly she seethed. That he no longer seemed angry only made Searle more so. Her hand shook slightly as she fit her key inside the lock and turned it.

Before she could push open the door, Buck captured her free hand. She tried, but failed, to snatch it back. His grip tightened and he ran his thumb over the center of her palm in a way that made her mouth go dry.

"I meant it, Searle," he said quietly.

She refused to look at him. Tingles were dashing from her palm to her heart. "Meant what?" she managed to ask.

"I will not hurt you. And I am persistent," he answered in a voice that caressed her like a kiss.

She yanked her hand and this time he let it go. She pushed into her apartment and slammed the door, knowing he was still there watching her.

CHAPTER EIGHT

Entering her office the following morning, Searle purposefully descended upon the bright bouquet atop her file cabinet. *You,* she mentally accused, *are the symbol of my moment of madness.* Before she had an opportunity to talk herself out of it, Searle swept up the bouquet and dumped it into her wire wastebasket, cut green vase and all. They were wilting anyway, she told herself as she kicked the basket out of sight behind her desk, then wondered why she had to justify her action. With a dismissive shrug, she tore into her work with vigor.

During the night, rational reflection had reestablished her sensible outlook. Involvement with a guy like Buck only spelled Trouble with a capital T. Searle escaped that brand of trouble when she left home to enter college and had firmly placed emotional turmoil behind her by the time she began her career. She didn't intend to backtrack now.

She knew what she wanted out of life and it wasn't the type of disaster Buck Carlton could bring. He ought to have been a pitcher, she decided. He certainly knew how to throw a curve. But she wasn't about to be caught standing at the plate again. Last night had been a fluke, a moment of ridiculous weakness that would not be repeated. The potent sexuality, the devastating charm, the irresistible good looks, would just have to captivate someone else. Searle wasn't biting.

Gathering her typed notes together, Searle made a brief outline for the direction of her feature on Carlton, then began composing the framework of the story. As she worked, she felt the thrill rising within her whenever she was into something good. And she knew this piece was good. In her concentrated excitement, she didn't hear the rapid knock on her door.

"Hiya, baby!"

Searle looked up in dismay to find Norman standing before her desk, widely displaying his capped teeth and openly running his lackluster eyes over her.

"Just thought I'd find out how the ball game went the other night," he explained, coming around to perch himself on the corner of her desk. "Did you need any help with the technical aspects of the game?"

Sighing, Searle hit the OFF key on her IBM, then turned to face him. It was obvious Norman meant to be helpful and she couldn't just give him the brush-off, no matter how great the temptation.

"No, Norm, I didn't. Thanks anyway. The game was as boring as I'd expected, but I got some color for the feature. I'm working on it now," she added, hoping he would get the hint. He didn't.

"What you needed was somebody there to explain it, you know, honey, add some fun," said Norman with one of his patented smiles.

"Really, I had no difficulty understanding baseball," she returned, her voice dropping several degrees in warmth. "And the story isn't really about the game, except how it shapes Carlton's life."

Norman's grin seemed fixed permanently in place. Searle wondered how long he'd had to practice to learn to keep it set like that. She tapped the desktop impatiently. Didn't he have some work to do here at Midwest? "Look, Norm, did you want something?" she said tersely. "I hate to sound rude, but I really need to get back to work on this story."

"Well, honey, I was thinking how's about—" began Norm. Oh, no, thought Searle, not another date request. She was saved by the ringing of her phone, but before she

could answer it, Norm lifted the receiver and spoke smoothly into it.

"Midwest Publishing, Miss Delacorte's office." Norm's thin cheeks drew in with a soundless whistle, then with a sharp look at Searle, he asked loudly, "Hey, baby, you in for Bucky Carlton?"

Throwing Norm a severe frown, she took the receiver from him and rasped, "Hello."

"Who the hell is that joker?" demanded Buck.

"What did you want?" she asked in return.

In the seconds of silence that followed Searle would have given much to be able to divine his thoughts. When he at last spoke it was in a carefully toneless voice that gave nothing away.

"What I wanted was to let you know I'm doing an autograph promotion at Rumford's downtown at one and I thought you could meet me, watch the action. You know, research for your story."

After last night, Searle really did not want to chance seeing him again. But there were still some big holes in her feature, holes that the right questions could easily fill. The knowledge that she was onto a good feature, perhaps one of her best ever, prompted her to reply abruptly, "All right. When and where?"

"As soon as you can get to Rumford's," he answered promptly, as if he'd never doubted she would come. "I'll be waiting for you in the manager's office."

He hung up before she could tell him she had no intention of leaving immediately. Well, he could just wait, she thought defiantly as she dropped her end of the phone.

"You going out with him?" asked Norm on a jealous note.

Her irritation turned to ire and she faced him with hostility. "He invited me to view an autograph session at Rumford's. Not that it's any of your business! Now, if you don't mind, I've got work to do."

"Sure, babe, sure. Sorry about the interruption." Norm backed toward the door. He'd never seen her eyes slant in quite that way, nor heard her voice drip with such acidity. Knowing what a woman in a temper could do, he exited quickly.

As soon as the door closed, Searle ripped her typed sheet from her machine, inserted a fresh page, and hurriedly compiled a list of questions she wanted to put to Buck, leaving space for her notes on his answers. Then she covered her IBM and shoved papers into organized piles upon her desk.

She made a brief stop in the ladies' room. Staring into the brightly lit mirror as if mesmerized by her own reflection, she removed all the pins from her hair, sending it into a cascading mane that made her look younger, less severe. She brushed her hair until it was a lustrous sheen against the wine collar of her cream shirtwaist dress, then pretended not to notice the stares she elicited as she paused at the receptionist's desk to move her marker from IN to OUT.

As she drove into the heart of the city, Searle alternately scolded and excused herself. It only made sense, she told herself, to fight fire with fire. Carlton wasn't the only one capable of throwing a curve—she'd meet him today with feminine compliance, get her answers, then retreat rapidly from the ranks. She resolutely ignored the vibrant tingle of anticipation, the feeling of being dizzily alive. From the instant she'd heard Buck speak, her blood had seemed to surge with renewed force through her veins, but Searle refused to acknowledge her physical responses.

She found a parking space in a tiny pay lot and collected a ticket from a huge man whose face seemed to consist solely of a red visor cap and brown cigar smoke. She strode with her usual seductive composure through the glass doors of the gigantic department store, carefully concealing her inner eagerness as she rode the escalator to

the top floor. When she entered the store manager's office, she wore a cool, confident air. Propped casually against the wall, arms crossed over the front of his sky-blue sport shirt, Buck watched her with narrowed eyes, thinking of the passion lying hidden beneath that glossy surface.

A lanky, bespectacled man quickly introduced himself as the manager. She didn't even catch his name before he excused himself and eased out of the room. Searle discovered her palms were moist.

"So who was he?" asked Buck by way of greeting as the manager closed the door.

Her brow elevated slightly. "Are you referring to Norm?" she inquired in a voice torn between annoyance and a perverse satisfaction.

"If that's the jerk who answered your phone, then yes," he replied as he straightened with a supple movement that sent her pulses racing. He jerked forward a molded chair of bright orange plastic and gestured her into it.

Though she privately agreed with Buck's description, she felt compelled to defend her co-worker. "Norman Kraekor just happens to be the best advertising man at Midwest," she said as she sat. "I think you categorize people too quickly," she finished with a formally critical note.

"No," denied Buck in a serious tone. Stroking the tip of his moustache with his finger, he went on, "I'm quick to make up my mind about people, that's true. You have to be a quick thinker to play ball—making snap judgments where and when to throw, steal a base, that sort of thing. It rubs off into my personal life, too. It doesn't take me long to decide what I like or don't like."

Searle had thrown open her notebook and was furiously writing in her abbreviated longhand. A line of concentration furrowed her brow, and watching her, Buck drew in a long, silent breath.

"One thing I definitely like," he began, then stopped.

"Yes?" she prompted, glancing up at him with a businesslike expectation parting her lips.

"I like your hair that way," he finished with feeling, his eyes fastened on her mouth.

A faint trace of embarrassment softened the prominent planes of her cheeks. Searle had deliberately worn her hair down to achieve an effect. But his approval seemed to have ricocheted on her, heightening her light-headed sensation. Recovering, she withdrew her typed notes and asked him to tell her about the types of promotions ballplayers do. Buck obliged her and soon Searle had gone through her entire list of questions. She took thorough notes and as she finished the last of them, she bestowed upon him a smile of real gratitude.

Her goodwill toward him lasted through the autograph session. An entire section of the sportsclothes department on the first floor had been provided for Blues' caps, T-shirts, jackets, socks, even jogging suits. Observing from the edge of the scene, Searle soon understood why Buck was one of the most popular players. Every person who jammed into the section—and she'd been surprised at the number of adults as well as children who came to see him—received Buck's attention. He took time to speak with as many as he could, always smiling and laughing, no matter how much he was jostled by the swelling crowd. He especially made time for the children, often demonstrating his now-famous open batting stance and encouraging each youngster to try. Without understanding why, Searle knew a feeling of pride as she watched him.

Though Buck was scheduled for an hour, he stayed twenty minutes over before allowing the store manager to escort them back to his office. Shoving his glasses up the bridge of his nose, the manager thanked Buck, then discreetly departed, leaving them standing alone by his desk.

"That was really impressive," said Searle warmly. "I'm glad I came along. Thanks for asking me."

Her inexplicable pride added a depth to her words and Buck reacted with a sudden, searing look of passion that robbed her of all breath. He took a step forward and she knew she would not resist. She wanted his touch, his kiss. But catching sight of a pie-faced clock on the wall, he halted.

"Damn," he muttered. He glanced at his watch. "Double damn."

"What's wrong?" she asked, feeling unbelievably frustrated.

"I've got to get over to the park for batting practice. Look, I'll save that third-base seat for you, but tonight you leave in the eighth inning and—"

"But I'm not going to tonight's game," she cut in with a smile.

He shot her one quick, hard look. "Sure you are. And I figure the way to avoid the problem we had on Tuesday is to—"

"I really can't go," she again interrupted. "I'd like to, Buck, but I'm already committed for tonight." She found herself wishing she hadn't agreed to attend the baby shower for Millie, the receptionist at Midwest. To her great surprise, she no longer wanted to avoid Buck; she wanted to go to the game.

Buck was staring at her with an unreadable expression, his brown eyes glinting. Then he stated flatly, "You're going out with Norman."

She almost laughed. She felt a strange, totally new elation and could not resist asking, "Surely you're not jealous?"

He shook his head in impatient denial. "Me? I'm not the jealous type. At least," he added with wry insight, "I never used to be. Just what is this guy to you, Searle?"

About to inform him that Norm was precisely nothing to her, Buck took her breath away by abruptly adding, "All right, go out with him if you must. But just don't go to bed with him, Searle. Right now, it wouldn't be fair to any of us, least of all you."

Her mouth dropped open. She tried to find words, but for seconds could only sputter. Absolute astonishment gave way to a much stronger, pulsating reaction. She couldn't believe he would assume such things about her, that he would take such rights upon himself. He stood, for once without a smile, waiting for her response. Well, she'd give him a response, all right. Her palm flashed out before either of them realized it and sounded sharply as it abruptly met his cheek.

Still burning, her hand hung in the air between them as they stared at each other in disbelief. Searle saw the red imprint on his face turn white. She was appalled at her own lack of control. Then, suddenly, unexpectedly, Buck laughed with a triumphant tilt of his head. He had finally managed to break through to her emotions in a very fundamental way and a stinging cheek seemed more than worth it to him.

Not understanding this, Searle saw Buck laughing at her. She felt mortified with herself and furious with him. And worse, much worse, she felt afraid of what it all meant. Without a word, before he could stop her, she spun and wrenched open the door. It quivered as she slammed out.

She drove back to Midwest Publishing in a jumble of confused emotions. Shock and fear were at first overridden by a smoldering rage. As it slowly drained from her, Searle coldly examined the implications of her actions. She felt shaken to her very depths, filled with disgust at her failure to maintain control over her temper. Never had she hit a person in anger. Never had she felt such anger. She knew from experience that anger was as dangerous as any other emotion and her stomach clenched. As if from some disembodied view, she pictured over and over her hand cracking against Buck's cheek. It made her feel sick.

She was trembling as she returned her marker to the IN position. Dimly, she heard someone speaking to her and realized Millie was reminding her about tonight. The cheery receptionist was one of the few people in the company with whom Searle had daily contact, and Millie's warm, bubbly nature had broken down some of her reserve. In her own noncommittal way, Searle liked the younger girl.

"I won't forget, Millie," she forced herself to reply. "Hold all my calls this afternoon. I don't want to be disturbed."

In a zombielike trance, she returned to her office, numbly sat down, and placed her hands palm down on her desk. She knew she must not allow herself to see him again. No matter how she fought it, no matter how she argued against it, she couldn't seem to stop herself from responding to Buck Carlton. It was all physical, she knew that, but it played havoc with her peace of mind. She didn't want to give in to her feelings, not now, not ever. She had just come too close to getting burned and she knew better than to continue playing with the matches.

She forced herself to think of something else. She concentrated on the evening ahead. The shower would be a rare occurrence for her. Since her parents' deaths while she was still in college, Searle's social contact with people had been limited. Fiercely independent, lacking the need to surround herself with others, she had never encouraged acquaintances to become anything more. Her reserve was often mistaken for an attitude of superiority, and Searle, afraid to commit herself to any emotional relationship, had done nothing to correct this impression.

Recently, however, there had been a nagging emptiness about her life that Searle had been reluctant to acknowledge. She wondered if the same feeling that had prompted her to accept the shower invitation had not also been responsible for her subconscious encouragement of Buck

Carlton. It was an arresting thought and one that she wasn't ready to face. She turned back to her work with a grim determination not to think at all.

Late that afternoon, as she was clearing her desk, getting ready to leave for the weekend, her phone rang. Realizing it must be Lenn on the interoffice line, Searle picked it up before it could ring again.

"Been waiting for my call?" came the immediate greeting.

"How did you get through?" she demanded brusquely, grappling with the totally unwanted hammering of her heart.

"Oh, I have my ways," Buck replied in a voice oozing with cocky masculinity.

"I'm sure you have," she agreed acidly. She wondered precisely which way he employed to get around Millie. "I was just on my way out."

"Yeah, I know you're in a hurry to get on with the big evening," he said lazily. Searle instantly wished she knew if he'd learned where she was really going. "But, Searle, I just wanted to remind you that I'm a very persistent guy."

"You don't say," she remarked dryly.

"I do. Think of me tonight."

And then he hung up. Searle slammed the phone down and stood glaring at its offensive shape. No way was she falling for his power of suggestion. Buck Carlton was going to be the last thing she would think about tonight.

But, of course, thoughts of the big lug elbowed their way into her mind throughout the evening. Try as she might, Searle couldn't dispel the image of him, not even during the party for Millie.

When she arrived, Searle was cornered by Millie and greeted with an apologetic smile. "I hope you weren't angry that I let that last call go through."

"Of course not, Millie," she said smoothly.

The short, extremely round woman brushed straying auburn hair from her freckled face and said with a laugh, "I really didn't mean to, but he kept calling and calling. Every half hour all afternoon! Finally, he told me that a woman with a voice as sexy as mine—"

So that's how he did it, thought Searle with a clinical interest.

"—would just have to be sympathetic to a man's needs and he claimed that what he needed was to speak with you."

"Oh?" inquired Searle in a voice void of warmth.

"Yes," laughed Millie self-consciously. "Well, how could I not let him after that?" Her look and laugh mingled apology with curiosity.

Searle satisfied only the apology, setting Millie's mind at ease on the score of letting the call go through. But her own mind was in a turmoil for the rest of the evening. As she mechanically joined in the laughter and half attended to the chatter surrounding her, she faced the realization that, just as he had said, Buck Carlton was indeed a very persistent guy.

CHAPTER NINE

Waking with a languid stretch into the threads of morning light meandering over her pillow, Searle discovered the turmoil within her had stilled. Her serene confidence had again reasserted itself, and as she repeated the lazy extension of her limbs, she smiled over yesterday's emotional upheaval. Must have been the full moon, she decided, yawning. Makes people do things absolutely foreign to their natures. Like overreacting to supremely sensual males bent on seduction. It was a classic case of losing one's sense of proportion. Viewing it as such, Searle rose to meet the day with a firm assurance that her sense of proportion stood solidly in place.

Her self-satisfaction carried her through the morning. As usual on Saturdays, Searle donned an old pair of shorts with frayed cuffs, and a thin halter-top, then swept her mass of hair precariously upward, clamping it into place with one large clip. The tousled knot, with stray tendrils tumbling this way and that, was nothing like the sleek, severe roll she wore to work. The casual style emphasized the unique beauty of her asymmetrical cheeks while adding a vulnerability she did not otherwise allow to be seen.

Two cups of coffee later, Searle began to clean her apartment. The routine never varied. She started in her bedroom and worked toward the living room. Since everything was neatly arranged and cleaned weekly, it was scarcely two hours later when she was winding the cord around the canister body of her small vacuum. There only remained shopping and laundry before the rest of her weekend was free.

Blowing a loose wisp of hair off her forehead, she wrote out a neat, thorough list of her grocery needs. The sun streamed brightly into the room, spreading a gleam over her polished glass-and-chrome tables and beckoning her outside. She decided against changing; her list wasn't that long and it looked like a typically hot, humid late July day out there. And, of course, there was still the wicker basket full of laundry to be done when she returned.

She had been right. It was hot. The humidity closed around her with enervating effect as she stepped out of her air-conditioned apartment into the open-air hallway. She instantly decided the most active thing she'd be doing this afternoon was lifting a book to read. Even a short walk through the park would leave one dripping in this weather. How did ballplayers manage in this heat? she wondered, then resolutely told herself she really didn't care.

Walking the linoleum aisles at the supermarket, carefully selecting only those items included on her list, Searle wheeled her steadily filling basket into the liquor department. As she moved purposefully toward the wines, she noticed a young couple strolling languorously ahead of her, locked arm-in-arm. The sight filled Searle with a longing she'd never known before, and the empty ache inside her grew despite her efforts to shut it off. Grabbing a bottle of sparkling white wine without even looking at it, she turned her cart into the nearest check-out lane. It was only as she was driving home that she remembered that the last item on her list had not been purchased. She wondered if her sanity was intact. She decided to look at the moon tonight and see just how full it still was.

Because her arms were full of groceries, she watched each step she took as she climbed the stairwell. As she reached the landing, however, she shifted the weight of her bags to her hips and raised her head. There he was, leaning casually into the wood of her door and filling the narrow hall space with his overwhelming masculinity.

He erased the space between them with his rugged grace, then took the bags from her arms. Peering over cellophane and celery sticks, Buck grinned boyishly and quirked his sandy brows. Searle's intention of telling him sternly to go away evaporated. She fumbled with her keys as she drew them from the pocket of her shorts, then unlocked her door.

Without a word, she held the door wide for him, shutting it as he passed through. He sauntered to the counter, dropped the brown sacks on it, then turned. His eyes darkened to a near-black as they ran the length of her, from the soft leather of her sandals to the rapidly disintegrating knot of her hair. Dark fire flamed within them as they rested on the beauty of her face, free of makeup and absurdly lovely.

Without the protection of her usual sophisticated clothes, Searle felt incredibly vulnerable, like a warrior caught in battle without armor. Words seemed to stick in her now-dry throat, lead seemed to weight her limbs. His eyes began to travel lazily back down her figure, spurring her into movement at last.

"Why must you always," she demanded as she strode into the kitchenette, "look at me as if you're about to devour me for dessert?"

"Is that how I look at you?" asked Buck, an arrested look on his face.

"Yes!" answered Searle emphatically. Pointing with the celery bunch she extracted from one bag, she added darkly, "All the time."

"It's your own fault, you know," he said, coming into the kitchen beside her. "If you wouldn't always look so damned appetizing . . ."

"Here! Make yourself useful!" ordered Searle tartly, shoving cans of tomato sauce at him and nodding toward a cupboard. As always, the warmth of his presence disturbed her in ways she couldn't define. Her senses seemed attuned so that his least action was communicated to her even when she refused to look at him. She fought against her reactions, succeeding in appearing remarkably poised.

"Did you have a good night?" inquired Buck casually.

She cast a quick, suspicious glance at him, but his head was turned into the shadows of the cupboard. "Yes, did you?" she returned evenly, pulling yet more cans from her sack and strewing them over the countertop.

"Don't you know?" Withdrawing from the shadows, he subjected her to a sharp, searching stare.

"No," she admitted. "Should I?" As she raised her eyes from the chore of folding up the bags, she witnessed a host of emotions play over his broad features. She readily recognized disbelief, then wondered if that could truly be a flicker of hurt as well. A need to explain prodded at her. "I don't read the paper until late on Saturday, Buck."

"I wondered before . . . don't you have a TV or stereo?"

"No, just a clock radio." As he shook his head in amazement, she went on, "I just haven't had the money yet for those luxuries. I don't believe in credit buying. Everything in here I paid for, in full, the day I bought it. And each piece came in one at a time after long months of saving and way too many yogurt lunches."

Buck's eyes circled the room, then came back to rest on the pride in her face. Nodding, he said sincerely, "You've accomplished a lot for yourself, Searle."

She found she could no longer trust herself to meet his gaze. She had expected some macho put-down, but he had once again thrown her off-balance, leaving her slightly confused and prey to unexpected emotions. As she busily finished stacking cans in their proper places, she said without looking at him, "I'm sorry about yesterday. I—I never meant to hit you."

"Actually, you know," he responded as he leaned against her dishwasher with studied nonchalance, "I'm rather glad you did."

"Glad!" she echoed, her head whipping up in astonishment.

"It proved you can react with honest passion. Not, of course," he qualified, "that I would tolerate a repeat performance."

"But I don't want to—" Searle swallowed the impulsive outburst. She couldn't tell him she didn't want to feel any passion—honest or otherwise—around him!

"Don't want to what?" he goaded lightly.

"Don't want to go around slapping people," she fenced, brushing past his intimidating form into the living room. It was difficult to maintain her usual cool, polite attitude with him towering over her meagerly dressed self, eyeing her as if she didn't have on even the bits of clothing she did!

"Oh, I don't think you need worry about it," said Buck with a smile that tilted his moustache crookedly. "I told you, I won't tolerate it again."

"*You* won't have anything to say about it!" she instantly returned in a voice thick with suppressed anger. From the safety of the living room, she sent him a glare worthy of a woman's scorn.

Gradually, he unfolded his muscular frame from the support of her dishwasher. His stance suddenly took on the menacing aspect of a king cobra poised to strike, and Searle involuntarily took a step backward.

"Oh, but I think I will, Searle," corrected Buck as he stood. "Someone's got to keep you in line. And for your information, I'm that someone."

As he moved into the living room, she thought it best to ignore his last remarks. Quickly forsaking her anger, she announced, "It's my day to clean and I still have laundry to do."

"I'll help," he said, leisurely following her as she turned toward the wicker basket. "Aren't you even interested?"

"In what?" she asked, lifting the basket as if to hide behind its protection.

"In how the game went last night, in how I did." Buck strolled up to her and suddenly she felt unaccountably dizzy. He took the basket from her unresisting hands, then walked to the door and paused expectantly.

"Oh, that. Yes, of course I am." Innate caution covered her heady excitement with a dull, flat intonation.

"God, what you do for my ego should be a crime," he commented with a wry, twisted smile. A matching twist seemed to wrench her heart, but Searle managed to remain outwardly calm as she gathered up the box of soap and fabric softener before leading him out.

"Did you hit a home run?" she asked. "Did your average stay above four hundred?"

"Yup."

"That's it? Yup?"

"Yup," he repeated. "You want details, you'll just have to read that sports page, lady."

She let herself laugh briefly as she led Buck downstairs. Her laugh was throaty and sensuously deep. The sooner he got rid of his armful of laundry, the better, he thought. The only thing he wanted his arms filled with was Searle Delacorte, every luscious inch of her. Unaware of her effect, concerned only with his maddening effect on her, Searle led him through a door behind the stairwell and down yet another flight of stairs, these covered by a rather threadbare carpet.

"The dreary depths of Pleasant Run Apartments," disclosed Searle as they reached the bottom of the steps.

Four white washing machines lined each side of the small room. A row of dryers hugged the end wall while a long formica counter was centered beneath the fluorescent light fixture. The linoleum floor, though clean, showed marks of wear. A travel poster tacked to one wall had done little to brighten up the typical laundry-room decor.

After setting the basket down, Buck stood back to let Searle begin sorting her laundry into two machines. The instant she dropped coins into the washers, he spoke. "Tell me about your night, Searle."

It was quietly said, but she realized from the tone and the determined expression to match it that Buck meant to have an answer. A severe mask covered her conflicting emotions and Buck, closely watching her, added tersely, "I know, you're going to tell me it's none of my damn business. But I'd like very much to make it my business."

"What do you mean?" she asked in sudden suspicion.

"You know what I mean," he replied curtly. Each low word grazed her as surely as his touch. "What did you do with Norman?"

"I—we—" she began, then stopped. Her first thought was an undeniable satisfaction over his obvious jealousy. It was quickly followed by a twinge of anger. He had no right to ask such things of her! "You were right. It's none of your business what I did last night," she ended on a sharp note.

The lids dropped over his eyes, hiding their expression from her. The muscle in his jaw flexed tensely, then suddenly Buck shrugged. He smiled ruefully. "Generally, I'm an even-tempered guy—"

"Oh?" broke in Searle, still hot. "You've certainly fooled me."

"Well, dammit, I am!" he returned in swift irritation. "But once in a while, I do something that totally blows my image—"

"Only once in a while?" she prodded with a cynical lift of her arched brows.

"Don't push me, Searle." He paused, then went on in a textured tone, "Last night was hell. I kept picturing you with him. I had to fight not to come by here after the game, but I knew what would happen if I saw you with him . . ." He let the words trail into the empty space between them.

The stretch of silence seemed to sap her strength to resist him. Her protective anger faded and Searle found herself speaking before she realized it. "Nothing would have happened, Buck."

The look on his face told her something damn well would have.

"I didn't go out with Norm last night," she explained simply, then immediately gave herself a mental kick for doing so.

He drew in a sharp breath. "You didn't?" he asked so softly she had to strain to hear it.

Wordlessly, Searle shook her head. Loose wisps of hair drifted across her cheek and she was intensely aware of his eyes as they followed the motion. She heard him take each breath as if it were painful for him to do so, and then with a will of their own, her eyes came up to meet his.

The disturbing dark flame that lit his gaze engulfed her in its white-hot conflagration. Unable to move, she watched with widened eyes as he stretched out his arm and traced the line of her bare shoulder with a gossamer touch. She shivered as his fingers lightly massaged the nape of her neck; her heartbeat quickened as he played with the knot of her halter-top.

"Searle," he whispered. "Searle."

Placing his other hand on the curve of her hip, he drew her against him. With a deliberate, slow-motion quality that seemed to strip away her ability to withstand him, his hand glided to the swirl of her hair, gently loosening the clip until the midnight mass spilled downward, veiling her cheeks. The coarse denim of his jeans rubbed the length of her bared legs, raising goose bumps of pleasure on them and making her every breath an effort.

"Melt for me, Searle," he commanded roughly.

"No," she weakly resisted, her voice paper-thin.

"I want you," murmured Buck into the dark cloud of her hair.

This isn't real, Searle told herself as she tried vainly to still the tremulous flutter of her heart. Staring beyond his shoulder at the row of white dryers, hearing the chugging rhythm of the washers, feeling the solid warmth of his muscled thighs, she wondered fleetingly if this were a surreal painting she'd somehow stepped into. *Men don't make passes in laundry rooms, do they?*

Apparently they did, for Buck's voice lowered to a near groan as, nibbling gently on her earlobe, he repeated, "I want you."

Suddenly, she knew that, more than anything, she wanted him, too. Her arms rose up to wreath his neck as her body arched into his, transmitting heated messages of desire between them. His lips moved with fierce hunger over the smooth plane of her cheek to crush against hers with a demanding passion that shook them both. His moustache chaffed her upper lip as his tongue sensuously explored the dark secrets of her mouth. His hands raced over her intimately, teasing her with brief, inflaming caresses.

For Searle, the excitement became unbearable. She felt devoured by an all-consuming, overpowering need. She had never felt such sweet torment and her body ached for him. Lacing her fingers into his hair, curving her body into his, she communicated the fullness of her mounting desire.

Abruptly, Buck pulled away, his eyes colored nearly black by his own matching need as he intently scrutinized her face. The composed mask was gone. He saw the emerald eyes sparkling with passion, the red lips puffed from his kisses, the slim nose flaring with quick, fervent breaths.

"Marry me, Searle. Now. As soon as possible," said Buck in a voice no longer steady.

Through the haze of her still raging desire, Searle

watched the squared lips move as he spoke. "What?" she breathed in disbelief.

"I want to get married," he replied thickly, capturing her against his chest once more. "To you. Immediately."

A rush of shock chased away the warm mists of her pleasure. For a long moment, she gazed unseeing at the mark just below the edge of his neck where the deep tan ended. Then, pushing herself a step away from him, Searle stared in escalating horror at Buck's face. The last of her passion receded before the tide of emotion she saw there and she brought her lips together with a snap.

"Are you crazy?" she demanded. "We've scarcely met! We don't even know each other!"

"I know enough to know I want you," said Buck, his voice still rough with desire. "I know I want to marry you. Does it really matter whether it's been days, weeks, or years?"

"Yes, it does!" she answered shakily. She took another step backward. *Marriage.* The very word repelled her. She felt suddenly cold, intensely and bitterly cold. She had nearly let the physical impact of this man carry her away into the sort of entanglement she'd always dreaded. The knowledge of her weakness froze her solid. "I don't want to be married to any man," she stated stiffly, "and least of all to one so completely different from me."

"Oh, hell," Buck muttered as his own passion ebbed. Running a hand through his hair, he regarded Searle with a look almost apologetic. He smiled crookedly and her disobedient heart lurched. "This isn't what I meant to do. I meant to be patient, to give you time to warm to the idea of me. But I guess I couldn't wait. I want you too much. I want you wearing my ring, sharing my life."

He saw the color drain completely away from her face, saw her withdraw further into her shell as her body went rigid. He silently swore, then said aloud in coaxing tones, "What's wrong, Searle? Tell me why you're retreating behind that wall of yours again. If it isn't because some guy burned you badly, then what is it? Tell me, Searle! I must know!"

The coaxing became an open plea, but Searle refused to be touched by it. With her head bent and her hands clenched tightly together, she said in a strained voice, "I told you. I have other plans for my life—my career—and I don't want to be sidetracked by a man."

"Any man? Or just me?" he asked sharply.

"Any man." Her toneless reply was accompanied by a flick of her green eyes. She knew she was lying. There was only one man capable of sidetracking her. He stood tensely, as if poised to recapture her into his arms. She had to avoid that at all costs. He made it too difficult for her to remain detached when he touched her. Her physical response to him was a danger she wasn't able to deny.

"What then?" repeated Buck. "What makes you look so stricken when I speak of marriage?"

"I don't look stricken," she denied, trying to keep her voice clear, throwing her head up to face him directly at last.

"Yes, you damn well do," he insisted through his teeth. "Behind all the frozen glitter of your eyes you do. Why? You must tell me why, Searle!"

He took a step toward her and she quickly moved another step back, shaking her head in mute refusal. He halted, looking at her with a perplexed hurt in his sable eyes that somehow hurt her, too. She had to end this probing before it totally stripped away her veneer of cold protection and exposed her to all the vulnerable emotions she kept so firmly locked away.

"Please, Buck, let's just drop this—"

"Like hell," he snapped. "I know damn good and well you can be warm enough when I get my hands on you." He caught the dark glint that threaded her eyes before she looked away and he pressed on harshly. "I'm not about to pretend I don't want you and you haven't yet given me any reason to drop the issue. Why can't we get married?"

She stared down at the floor. She knew that if she answered honestly, "I don't want to get hurt," he would brush away her fears. He was forceful, determined, and he would bulldoze right through her excuses, never understanding the myriad of reasons that made her believe her choice to remain emotionally isolated was the right choice. Even if she thought he would understand, Searle couldn't bring herself to speak of her parents. The wound went too deep to bear exposure and she would never willingly reveal it. She had to give him sensible, solid reasons or he'd go right on torturing her. Slowly, she raised her eyes.

"We have practically nothing in common," she said flatly. "We'd get along about as well as—as—" she floundered, searching for the correct simile or metaphor or whatever the hell it was she wanted.

"As husband and wife," supplied Buck. In a soothing tone, he went calmly on, "We have plenty in common, Searle, if you'd only let yourself see it. What's the real reason? Why are you still running scared?"

"Stop it!" she cried out. "Please," she added more quietly, attempting to maintain her control. Twisting her hands together, betraying her agitation, she declared, "How many times must I say it? I don't want marriage. I'm a—a career person. My job is the most important thing to me and—"

"And I won't interfere with that part of your life. I'd be proud to have a wife who's a success in her own right, Searle."

The washers charged into their spinning action, surrounding them with a noisy hum. Searle forced her hands to cease moving. Somehow, she had to make Buck understand that, for her, this was purely a physical attraction, nothing more.

"Buck, you've had plenty of women," she began hesitantly.

"Is that it? You're worried about my reputation?" Relief underscored his raw tone. "I thought I explained all that."

"Oh, come now," said Searle, grasping at the lifeline he was throwing her, "You can't pretend to me that you didn't earn your reputation. As a journalist, I know better than to believe the media invented all those tales, that you're a misunderstood innocent."

He again ran his hand through his hair, ruffling the dark layer beneath the gilded blond. "I'm thirty-one years old, for God's sake! I admit I've had women—enough of them over the years. Celibacy isn't in my nature, Searle."

She bent her head, turning away. Now, why did that pierce? It couldn't matter to her . . .

"How old are you?" growled Buck in sudden exasperation.

"Twenty-five. Which should convince you that I'm old enough to know what I want out of life," she answered, returning to her icy hauteur.

"Do you claim to be as pure as you were on day one?" he demanded. Her eyes widened, then narrowed, emphasizing the catlike slant. It was all the reply he needed. "I don't give a damn about your past, so why grill me about mine? It's the future—our future—that I care about, Searle! I want to be the only man in your life from now on, the man who cares for you, makes love to you."

The incessant clamoring of her pounding pulse roared in her ears. The washers had stopped, but neither noticed. Somehow, Searle had to make him stop pressing her before she did something they would both regret for the rest of their lives. He couldn't possibly understand how soul-shattering the daily torment of a mismatched marriage could be. Her heart was thudding with a painful precision as she forced her lips to move, her voice to work.

"Can't you get it through your head? Or is it too much of a blow to your oversized ego to accept the fact that I don't want to be your wife?" she asked acidly. "Well, accept it, Buck! Accept the fact that I don't love you."

A quiet confidence returned to Buck's stance, a virile lift of his lips quirked the ends of his moustache. "You can say that after what has passed between us? Your body tells me differently, Searle."

"That's just it!" she pounced swiftly. "That's just a physical reaction—"

"It will lead to loving," broke in Buck, his voice sensuously low once more. "I'll make you love me, Searle."

"You won't make me do anything!" she instantly retorted, then retreated with hurried steps as he appeared ready to prove his point then and there. "I don't *want* to love you!" she threw at him. "In fact, I hate you!"

She realized she was shouting and stopped, aghast. She never raised her voice, never! Her hands flew to cover her ears, her eyes skewered shut as if to shut out the reality around her. Searle hated loud arguments, she hated any vehement emotion. Her own quick temper had always been contained within a tight limit, but both yesterday and today she'd lost control in ways that made her feel sick.

She felt herself shaking, unable to still the trembling of her limbs. A numbing cold ran through her, deadening her to everything around her. Her hands were pried from her ears and forced down.

"Look at me, Searle," commanded Buck, gripping her hands tightly in his.

His voice came dimly to her, as if from some faraway place. Her lids slowly lifted. She saw him looking at her, concern softening the brown of his eyes. His harsh intake of breath told her that her eyes showed only indifference.

"You've got to risk loving sometime, Searle," said Buck with a razor-edged hiss. "You've got to risk living!"

Now was the time. Now she had to do it or give herself

over to the kind of lifelong misery her parents had so brutally inflicted on each other. With a piercing, frigid, icicle stab, she told him, "You may be right. Maybe I will. But one thing is certain. I will never take such a risk with you. The very idea is ludicrous. How could you possibly think I could ever relate to a jock like you?"

It was the clinical coldness of her rejection that hurt him. The precise, unemotional words tore at him, and for Buck, the elastic finally stretched too far. Every vestige of warmth passed from his expression and he released her hands with a jerk that jarred her. His raw temper serrated his cold tone when he finally replied.

"How could I indeed? I guess I forgot you're incapable of it. You've been too damn busy rating men to relate to them."

The stillness of his anger upset Searle far more than any amount of violence could have done. She flinched beneath his hard gaze, the taut cord in his neck telling her how rigidly he was controlling himself. Abruptly, he pivoted and walked away.

Numbly, from the depths of her self-imposed detachment, Searle turned to watch him mount the stairs. She heard the door above slam shut, then forced herself to move toward the washers. Opening the lids to pull her wet laundry out, she discovered her hands were shaking uncontrollably. Gripping the edge of the machine to steady herself, she drew in several sharp breaths.

"Better now," she said aloud. "Better to suffer a little now than a whole lot after being trapped into really loving him. Isn't it? Isn't it?"

Her question echoed shrilly, unanswered.

CHAPTER TEN

By the following Wednesday morning, the first sharp stabs of pain had dulled to an occasional blunt throb. The days had dragged by with a depressing sameness that Searle tried to persuade herself was not due to the absence of Buck Carlton. When he had left on Saturday, Searle had been shocked by the depth of her keen sense of loss. She'd hurt like hell inside and no amount of rationalization had eased the aching. She told herself it was a good thing she hadn't allowed him to touch her heart, because then the pain would have been unbearable . . .

She blamed her stark feeling of emptiness on physical frustration and convinced herself that she had done the right thing. Her way was the sensible way. Or so she told herself as she gulped down her morning coffee without really tasting it. Unable to stand the solitude of her apartment, she left for work early, refusing to think of anything beyond the beauty of the thin wispy clouds trailing in the clear morning sky as she drove. At Midwest, she thrust her marker to IN with unnecessary force and retreated to the refuge of her office to avoid the prework chatter sessions. Taking the chair at her desk, her heart pitched wildly.

A square white envelope stood propped against her telephone. Laying aside her purse, Searle reached for it with a hand that trembled. *Buck, oh Buck,* she thought with a soaring hope, *how do you manage these things?* Gold letters spelled out "Thank You" in script on the small card within and Searle's galloping heartbeat downshifted to low as she opened it to read, "Bob and I thank you for the lovely bunting for the baby . . ."

She didn't bother to read the rest of Millie's message but

crumpled the card with sudden, fierce defiance. How could she be so stupid? Once and for all, Searle Delacorte, get it through your head that it is over and done with. You should rejoice. You do rejoice.

For the umpteenth time since Saturday, she indulged in pondering "what-if." What if she had let Buck go on kissing, touching, loving her that night at his place? What if she had let Buck take her out Friday after the game? What if she had agreed, insanely, to marry him? But there were no what-ifs to change the implacable fact that it was over. There had been a finality to the hard look of pity Buck had thrown her with his last biting words. Why on earth wasn't she celebrating her near escape?

The problem, she had decided during one of her long nights, as she tossed and turned in a vain effort to sleep, was Buck himself. Beyond the sheer physical magnetism of him, beyond the way his body cried out its need for hers, he had had the gall to be none of the things she had expected. He had not been gauche, coarse, or intellectually underdeveloped. Further, though he reeked with a sexuality that fairly shouted "all-male," he did not seem to equate masculinity with superiority, despite his obvious manly determination to get his own way.

It had occurred to Searle that it was, perhaps, this determination that had prompted Buck to propose. He'd made it clear he wanted her and he was a man used to having what he wanted. Especially from women. She had been cool, unreceptive to his advances, at least compared with what she imagined to be the usual reception he got from her sex. Perhaps he'd come to think an offer of marriage would get her for him. She wondered what he would have done had he known of her willingness to give in to him physically. But she herself had only now come to understand how much she had actually wanted Buck, and the revelation was startling.

Her few forays into the realm of physical lovemaking

back in college had left her wondering what the big deal was about. It seemed to her then to be an absurdly awkward, somewhat ridiculous exercise. Over the years, she'd never felt the least wish to repeat the experiment. Then Buck Carlton had come along, making her tingle for his least touch, ache with the need for his kiss. She had suddenly realized that it might be exciting to make love to a man.

Forcing her mind away from the dangers of further such reflections, Searle worked listlessly through the morning. Shuffling the Carlton feature to the end of her "must-get-to" pile, she concentrated on routine articles that would keep her thoughts strictly on neutral ground. She was finally about to tackle the interview with grim determination when her phone rang.

It was Lenn, barking at her to come see him at once. *Saved by the bell,* she thought wryly as she strode out of her cubicle.

She found Roberts outside his office, bending over a slanted table with Jeff Johnson, the company's design artist. When Searle came up, both men glanced briefly at her, then continued discussing the design of the September layout. Stabbing a finger at a page on the table, Lenn remarked disparagingly on Johnson's use of a six-inch border, baldly ordering him to tone it down to at least a four-inch, for God's sake. Searle smiled slightly as Jeff nodded; it was obvious Lenn was in his most despotic mood.

Still soundly contradicting the artist's conceptions, the editor shot a sudden, sharp look at Searle from behind his gold-rimmed glasses, taking note of her wan features. Lack of sleep over the past few nights had marked her. Heavy shadows ringed her eyes, throwing the upward slant into emphasis and making the rest of her angular face appear gaunt. With a dismissive nod to Johnson,

Roberts moved briskly into his office, waving Searle into the chair across his desk as he did so.

"Are you feeling sick?" Lenn demanded as soon as she sat down.

"No," she replied with a shrug. Certainly not heartsick.

"Are you up to taking a trip?" he questioned abruptly.

"Why?" she asked in return.

"How's the Carlton piece going?" queried Roberts instead of replying. His voice was even, giving nothing away.

"I'm near to wrapping it up," answered Searle flatly.

Lenn's eyes narrowed. He had no doubt that something was wrong, but he wasn't the man to pry. He kept his concern out of his voice when he said briskly, "Well, I think it can be added to—this story has gotten bigger with the way Carlton's playing. This last weekend really decided me."

She looked momentarily shocked. *How could he know what had happened Saturday?* was her first, wild thought. Then, more calmly, she realized he must be referring to something else. "This weekend?" she responded cautiously. "Decided what?"

"The way Carlton's been playing," repeated Lenn dryly. "They're calling him 'Mr. Aggressive' now and I think we should capitalize on all the publicity he's generating. I'm upping the print on the September issue, so I want this feature to be as in-depth as possible. That's why I'm sending you to New York."

"You're what?"

Noting with a satisfied smile that he had her full attention at last, the editor leaned casually back and expanded. "I'm sending you to New York. Thought you could cover the games they're playing there, and more important, talk with some of the other players, get some usable quotes about their views of their teammate. And, of course, find out how all the publicity, the pressure of continuing to hit is affecting Carlton."

Breathlessly, very casually, Searle inquired, "Has this been cleared with Carlton?"

"No," returned Lenn, propelling her heart back into the dull thud it was becoming accustomed to. "But the Blues' public relations director has been very cooperative to the hometown mag; in fact, he's arranged for you to have a room in their hotel. He's probably passed the info along to Carlton. Right after the New York series, I want you to get back here and give me that story."

"Fine," she said dully. For one brief instant, she'd thought Buck had somehow been behind this. The knowledge that he had nothing to do with it should have been a relief. It wasn't.

Briefly, Lenn sketched the outline for her trip. She was to leave on a flight tonight and go directly to the hotel where she would be contacted by the Blues' traveling secretary. Tickets for games two and three of the series would be provided, though not in the press box. A match had been lit under the media and in the midst of the bonfire, Carlton was consumed by the national press. Still, she would have an edge by being in the same hotel and having access, courtesy of the Blues' front office, to the players.

As he spoke, the unnatural lethargy that had enveloped her for days began to drain from Searle. Her pulse quickened, her eyes began to glow attentively as a strange elation took hold of her, an elation that carried her from Lenn's office directly to her apartment to begin packing. She tried half-heartedly to convince herself her spiraling spirits weren't due to the prospect of seeing Buck again, but gave up the attempt as she selected, folded, and packed her clothes.

She began to picture their meeting. She wondered if Buck would still want her and knew that if he did, she would not resist. Her physical need for him had grown too great for her to worry about being simply another of Carlton's conquests.

Although Buck had said he wanted to marry her, Searle did not accept it, believing instead that he'd have soon tired of her had she fallen directly into his arms like every other woman he met. It was the challenge of her that had brought about Buck's proposal, she was certain, and once he knew he could have her without it, he would undoubtedly forget all about marriage.

A shudder uncontrollably shook her and she paused before closing her carry-on bag. There was no danger, she sternly reminded herself. After all, this was just a physical thing, wasn't it? No danger of getting her heart involved, was there? The desire to once, just this once, discover what she was capable of feeling, if only on the physical level, had become an obsession. And giving herself to Buck Carlton was the only cure.

By the time she threw her bag into her car, Searle had begun to feel light-hearted. Excitement vibrated within her at the thought of seeing Buck again and the nightmare of his last words and last look finally began to fade. Driving the winding stretch of freeway to the airport without seeing any of the lush summer greenery, she wondered ironically what Lenn would have said about his "passionless professional" if he could know she was coldly contemplating an affair with her latest interviewee. His imagined response wrung a spontaneous laugh from her and she was still smiling when she boarded her flight.

Although it was the first full meal she had eaten in several days, Searle was only barely aware of the chicken dinner served in-flight. Her mind was filled with Buck and had no room for anything as mundane as food. Far too exhilarated to doze, she stared out the small cube of a window into the black void that was the night sky, occasionally catching her own vague reflection shimmering back at her. Again and again, she envisioned the moment when she would explain to Buck how she wanted him, how she was willing to give herself to him, and how he would wrap her into his strong arms.

Such visions filled her with a delirious, drunken sensation that had nothing to do with the wine she drank on the flight. Having come to her decision to let her physical defenses down, Searle was eager to act upon it. She couldn't unbuckle her seat belt fast enough when they finally touched down at La Guardia. She smiled sincerely at the stewardess, who wished her a good time in New York as she stepped off the plane and strode down the runway.

Her sense of intoxicated impatience grew during the taxi ride to the hotel. Without so much as a glance at the bustling activity jamming the street around her, Searle paid the cabby and briskly entered the hotel lobby. The elegance of subdued lighting and hushed voices permeated despite the constant movement of people across the carpeted floor. She ran her eyes over the marbled staircase and mirrored walls, remembering Buck's joking statement that on the road, his main off-field activity was lobby sitting. But of course, he wasn't there. He'd be at the ball park. A quick check of her watch told her the game would already be in progress.

At last the bellboy arrived to escort her to her room. She rode the elevator up and took the flat plastic card that was her room key in silence, not trusting her voice to remain steady, even with the bellboy. Green and yellow flowers bedecked the curtains and the full-sized bed; marble topped the nightstand and low vanity, but essentially the small square room bore the same impersonal look of all hotel rooms. Searle dropped her purse and carry-on onto the thick cushion of the one chair and marched purposefully toward the phone.

She made three calls. The first, a message for Mr. Carlton, simply leaving her name and room number. The second, a call to inform Will Thompson, the Blues' road secretary, that she'd arrived. The third was to the front desk to discover if there was a cable channel on which she could watch the baseball game. There was. Following careful instructions, she tuned in and watched as she hung up her clothes and changed into her robe.

It was apparent that Buck Carlton was indeed the golden boy of baseball. The commentators provided more than enough information about him, his hitting streak, and his aggressive style of play, to satisfy Searle's need to see as much of Buck as possible. During a brief close-up interview, she sat immobile, drinking in his every word, every movement. As she watched his moustache twitch upward with his boyish grin, saw his velvet-brown eyes sparkle mischievously, followed his hand as it ruffled his sun-kissed hair, Searle ached with overwhelming desire.

Once, she actually reached out and stroked the image smiling at her on the screen. With a self-conscious laugh, she snatched her hand away, as though observed doing something foolish. The sooner she could get Buck Carlton into her arms, she then realized, the sooner she'd get over this physical obsession she could not otherwise escape. The affair would undoubtedly be brief—with Carlton, it always was—but she hoped desperately it would get Carlton out of her system.

At last the game was over, another Blues' victory in a season that seemed impossible for them to lose, and Searle's pounding anticipation increased. Checking her travel clock, she decided to shower and change, then wait for Buck to come or call, as she was certain he would when he got her message.

He did neither. When her clock declared it to be well past midnight, Searle finally gave up expecting him. She slowly undressed, hanging up her jonquil sundress with hands that shook. A fear that he did not intend to contact her mounted, refusing to be damped down. With one last glare at the silent phone, she slipped into the crispness of her bed and lay listening to the cacophony of the New York night twenty-two stories below.

She told herself that he had been delayed, that he would call in the morning. There was no reason, no reason at all, to feel this pressure on her chest, as if some invisible hand were pushing her heart down, down, down to the depths of her innermost self. Such fancies, combined with the shrill noises screaming up from the streets below, kept her from falling into anything more than a light doze and by morning, the circles beneath her eyes had darkened, giving her a vulnerable, little girl look she was not accustomed to.

Searle was sampling the continental breakfast delivered by room service when her phone rang. Heart knocking fitfully into her ribs, she answered it with a breathless "Hello."

"Ms. Delacorte?" inquired a bland male voice that instantly quieted her beating heart.

"Yes," she affirmed dully.

"I'm Will Thompson with the Blues. When will you be ready to start interviewing some of our players?"

"I'm ready now, Mr. Thompson," she said in that same toneless voice that matched her now-empty feeling.

"Good," he said immediately. "I'll be right up."

Thompson arrived at her door within minutes. His appearance was as bland as his voice, from his clipped brown hair to his conservative dark-blue suit, but his eyes glinted with appreciation as he led her to the suite he was using as a pressroom. Searle met the look without the least enthusiasm and heard his even monotone without knowing what it was he was saying.

That afternoon, she spoke to, seemingly, every player in the Blues' organization. Except one. The only one who mattered for her never appeared. She hid her disappointment behind the businesslike reserve that had always served her well in the past and elicited enough quotes for a few paragraphs. She hoped Lenn would be happy with it, because that appeared to be all she was going to get out of this trip. Though she checked with the front desk repeatedly, there were no messages left for her, and Searle now understood that Buck would not be contacting her.

Without at first admitting it, the sharpness of her disappointment shocked her. How had she come to let the big jock affect her this way? When she thought of how close she had come to risking herself, to telling him she wanted him, Searle nearly laughed with her relief over her escape. But she could not laugh. She had to do something to get the ape out of her system, something that would erase her ceaseless need to be near him.

As she sat at the ball park that night, a humid wind whipping through her loosened hair, Searle thought of her incessant need and shivered with a deathly inner chill. The hot July night could not warm her, nothing could warm her as she watched with bitter pain each movement Buck Carlton made on the field. One tiny part of her fueled her wavering hope by whispering "maybe tonight, maybe tonight," until she felt ready to scream with her frustration.

She had toyed with the idea of leaving another message for Buck, but pride had at least saved her from that foolish impulse. He was making it all too clear what he thought of her, and Searle knew now it was too late to tell him of her hidden desires.

She returned to the hotel not even knowing or caring who won the game. Several players and Will Thompson had asked her to stop in the hotel bar for a drink, but she resolutely declined. She firmly passed by the front desk, refusing to inquire again for the message she knew would not be there, and took the first available elevator up to her room. Like a sleepwalker, she mechanically prepared for bed, then tossed restlessly in the dark, willing herself to sleep, to forget.

CHAPTER ELEVEN

Searle stood by her window, curtain held back by one hand, and stared out at the sheet of rain that veiled the skyscrapers from view. The drizzly gray day had perfectly suited her doleful spirits, but when the intermittent drizzle gave way to drenching rain, a crushing depression settled over her. The long, empty hours of her dull day threatened to stretch through the night and Searle did not think she could endure it. She almost wished Will Thompson would call. He had made it plain in his reserved monotone that he was interested, but Searle hadn't been able to respond even politely to his flattering hints. Tonight, however, she would welcome him, anyone who would take her thoughts off a certain ballplayer for even one brief hour.

When the game was called, Searle met the news with a fatalist's shrug of acceptance. She ate a solitary dinner in one of the hotel's three restaurants, the brightest-lit, noisiest one, then retired to her room, where she called the airlines to confirm her morning flight reservation. She couldn't wait to leave, to get away from the scene of her mental humiliation. *Running scared?* she mocked herself as she stood at the window. She dropped the curtain and angrily spun to the closet. Desperate to do something, anything to snap out of the depression she was wallowing in, Searle changed into a violet cocktail dress with a caped top and circle skirt that dramatically draped her slender figure. With a touch of bravura, she let down her hair and vigorously brushed the midnight sheen until it haloed her face.

She would go out, she told herself with resolution, and celebrate. Celebrate the wrapping up of her story. The departure of Buck Carlton from her life. The return of her sanity. Celebrate.

Strapping high-heeled black patent sandals on her feet, she took one last look in the mirror. The only thing missing for a celebration was a bright smile. She stretched her lips. Well, it would have to do, she asserted, turning to leave. There was a bar downstairs, a bar that glowed with unnatural red light. It would be perfect. She was one step from the door when the knock came. She paused, then a welcoming smile lit up her face in earnest. So Will Thompson had come through in her hour of need after all.

She tugged open the door and her smile froze in place. Buck Carlton stood there, a wine bottle dangling casually from one hand.

"Well," he said, his eyes taking in each detail of her from beneath half-lowered lids. "Well," he said again, drawing the word out until it cloaked her with its velvet softness.

Searle did not move. She couldn't believe it. Having just convinced herself to accept Buck's exit from her life, here he was negligently disrupting her peace of mind with the subtlety of a volcano. Her heart sputtered, then began to knock tightly as she stared at him.

He looked as relaxed as ever, green-and-brown checked shirt tucked carelessly into tight denim jeans, the sleeves rolled haphazardly up to his elbow, exposing the fine dusting of golden hair along his forearms. Rumpled blond hair fell over his brow in a way that demanded a woman's hand smooth it back for him and Searle managed to restrain doing so only as she noticed the cocoa-dark eyes were gleaming at her with masculine amusement. She realized her mouth was hanging open and shut it with a little snap.

Grinning broadly, Buck abruptly pushed past her, kicking the door shut and sauntering into her room. After a brief hesitation, she followed him. Trying to sound as

offhand as he, she coolly asked, "What are you doing here?"

"I thought you wanted me here," he replied, both thick brows lifting. "Why else did you leave your name and room number?"

"That," she stated with slicing words, "was on Wednesday. In case you hadn't noticed, this happens to be Friday."

Without answering, he set the wine bottle atop the marbled dresser, then wandered past her into the bathroom. *I shall,* thought Searle in a blaze of emotions, *scream!* Then he emerged, a paper-wrapped glass in each hand, a smile tilting his expression, and Searle's emotions converged into one single burst of happiness.

"Don't tell me," he said with a distinct twinkle, "that you've been waiting for me for two whole days."

"I won't tell you any such thing," she quickly retorted.

"No?" he responded, flicking his eyes over her dress as he uncorked the wine. "So who were you waiting for?"

The cork flew into the air with a resounding pop and he turned to strip the paper from the glasses. As he filled them with the deep red liquid, she answered calmly, "I wasn't waiting for anyone."

"Sure you weren't," he agreed. Handing her a glass, he took a sip, then added sharply, "You always dress like this for an evening alone?"

"No," she laughed, feeling better and better with each word, each look he gave her. "But I was about to go to the bar for a drink to celebrate."

His eyes ran the length of her again, arousing all her senses to a pitch of exhilaration.

She looked, however, as regally cool as ever. Buck wondered why he had come. "Celebrate what?" he inquired, sounding slightly miffed.

"The wrapping up of my feature," she replied, eyeing him obliquely from the slanted corners of her eyes. She

didn't add, celebrate getting you out of my system, because, clearly, she hadn't. Trying to control the erratic pulsation of her blood, she sat on the edge of the Queen Anne chair and asked, "Why have you come? I'd gotten the impression you weren't going to."

His eyes searched her face, then he shrugged. "You were right. I really wasn't going to come to you, Searle," he said evenly. He refilled his glass, then tipped the bottle toward her. As she shook her head slightly, he propped himself on the rim of the vanity and studied her for a long, breathless moment. "I told myself I'd be a fool to come to you. But then something inside me said, 'Look, Bucky old boy, you can't just let her go on like that. If she keeps hiding from life, she'll miss the whole point of it and we can't have that, can we?' Naturally, I said, 'We sure as hell can and she damn well deserves it!' "

He took a sip of his wine, then looked intently into the burgundy liquid. Searle gulped down the last of her wine, wondering if she should dare tell him she felt ready to chance an affair. He spoke before she gathered her courage together.

"Then, again, it occurred to me that I'd a duty to perform."

"Duty?" she echoed blankly.

"Yup," said Buck, setting aside his empty glass. He stretched out a hand, she put her glass into it, and he set it beside his. Then he returned his hand to her. She stared at it dumbly for a second, then as if hypnotized by it, placed her own slim hand within its grasp. He pulled her up, then straightened to meet her as she came to him.

"You may not want me now, Searle Delacorte," he stated with the precision of a doctor making a diagnosis, "but, by God, you're going to want me. I'm going to make you want me."

His hands slid down her bare arms to the curve of her hips. Then, slowly, tantalizingly, they started teasing up-

ward along her spine, all the while pressing her closer into his hard muscles.

"I'm going to make you want me so much that you'll know what it means to ache with the need," he continued in chilling tones that belied the fire in his touch.

His fingers traced swirling patterns on her back with a lightness that left Searle dizzy, breathless. *Make me want you?* she thought through the haze of her mounting desire. *My body does want you!* She tried to translate the thought to words.

"Oh, Buck, I—"

His lips smothered hers, stealing the breath and the words from her in one swift demand. Searle's mouth parted in ardent response and she trembled as his tongue lightly caressed hers. "No more protests, Searle, no more denials," Buck rasped softly. "This time you'll melt for me."

Then the fierceness of his kiss swept away all her thoughts, leaving only sweet, soaring sensation. She was aware of nothing beyond the warmth of his breath as it mingled with hers, the heat of his muscled frame crushing against her soft curves, the moistness of his lips, the gentleness of his fingertips. She was stunned when he suddenly released her.

"Still feel like celebrating?" he asked with a tranquillity that shocked her.

She stood shaking as the blood pounded through her veins. His nearness left her legs weak, the gaze beneath his lowered lids burned as it traveled over her.

"Celebrating?" she repeated stupidly.

"Sure. I think we could take in a bar or two before curfew." With a hand upon the small of her back he steered her toward the door. She slowly regained a regular breathing pattern, but it wasn't until they emerged from the silent elevator ride that she overcame the urge to kick him. How could he turn off all that passion so abruptly?

Sitting in a deserted corner of the hotel bar, with the dull red glow burnishing his ruffled hair, Searle could only stare at him in wonder as he talked effortlessly about all the media hype over his hitting streak. It was as if he hadn't actually felt anything back in her room. The thought pierced her.

By sheer force of will, she shoved the pain away and summoned up a smile of interest. Through two rounds of drinks, they conversed lightly, easily. The undercurrent of sexual tension was stifled. Only once did it briefly emerge, when Buck halted in midsentence and leaned over the table to cup her hand in his.

"Are you wanting me, Searle? Are you thinking of my lips, my hands?" he whispered, so low she wondered if she had indeed heard the words.

He instantly removed his hand, straightened, and resumed talking for all the world as if he hadn't just inflamed every nerve inside her. She stared at his squared lips, which sent his moustache first one way then another as he spoke, and she remembered the soft prickle of it against her skin. Feeling the crimson heat mount her neck, she quickly lowered her eyes. There were his hands, one loosely wrapped around his glass, the other resting idly on the table. She felt again the quivers they had sent through her. A flush flared into her cheeks.

With a guilty start, she raised her eyes to meet his. Even in the dim light, she could see his amusement glint at her, she could see that he could read her visions and that he was enjoying her discomfiture. With a supreme effort, she forced herself to meet his gaze and continue conversing, just as if she weren't thinking solely of his magnificent body, his physical strength, and the power they had upon her.

As soon as she finished her second daiquiri, Buck settled the tab, then rose to escort her to the lobby.

"Well, where would you like to celebrate now?" he asked lightly.

"I think I'm done celebrating, Buck," she answered, stamping down her rising tense expectation and matching his tone. "I'd better retire for the night. I've an early morning flight to catch, and I can't oversleep."

"It's your party," he said, stopping before the elevator bank and pressing the button. "So you're going back tomorrow?"

"Yes."

With a soft ping, the elevator doors opened and they entered. As the doors closed upon them and they began to move motionlessly upward, Searle fought against a sudden panic. What if he didn't want to come in? Every end of her every nerve was tingling with excitement. If he didn't come into her room, how would she ever get over this obsessive need for him? She glanced sideways at him. He stood relaxed, a smile playing upon his lips, making no attempt whatsoever to touch her. She found herself wishing the elevator would jam and they'd be stuck together.

The elevator stopped and the doors opened, but Searle hesitated.

"Something wrong?" asked Buck in a taunting tone.

"No, of course not," she replied, following him out. How could she ask him if he meant to stay or not?

The tension in the narrow hallway escalated as they walked silently to her room. The buzz of the card inserted in the door reverberated in Searle's oversensitive ears. As she pushed it open, she turned, a smile of seductive invitation parting her lips.

"Thanks for helping me celebrate, Buck." Her voice, amazingly, remained even and cool. "Will you come in for a while?"

Searle's heart stopped beating as she waited for his answer. She could not believe she had actually invited him into her room; she could not believe how important his response had become to her.

"I'm afraid not," he said without expression. "We're on curfew, you know, and I wouldn't want my roommate wondering where the hell I'd got off to."

"Of course not," she agreed through stiff lips, feeling as if she'd been slapped. "Well, good night then."

"Good night," he responded, beginning to turn away. "Oh, Searle," he added, turning back to her and catapulting her heart into a frantic cadence.

"Yes?" she said, excitement shading her word.

"Have a good flight," he said. He turned and strolled away.

She shut the door heavily. *Damn him, damn him!* she silently raged as she threw down her clutch bag and tore off her shoes. Why would he never do what she expected of him? Any other man would have been rushing into bed with her an hour ago with the signals she'd been giving off. She'd practically stamped her forehead with a sign that read, "Take me, I'm yours," and he had deliberately, coldly, ignored it.

Why, she demanded of herself, did she let Buck Carlton upset her like this? Never had she throbbed with such a wanting, never had she felt so frustrated. Buck had played with her, teasing her, yet remained so removed that it hurt. With a sudden pang, Searle realized that it was usually she who remained detached and she knew a moment of guilty wonder. Had this frustrated need filled the men she had so coolly put off?

Not feeling quite ready to face the enormity of that concept, and angrier than ever with herself, she slapped her shoes back onto her feet. She would go back down to that bar and enjoy herself! She would not sit here and feel sorry for herself over some egocentric jock any longer. In a state of repressed fury, she snatched up her purse and wrenched open her door, only to stand face-to-face with Buck.

"I wondered how long it would take you to come after me," he said with a laugh that dripped male satisfaction.

"I wasn't coming after you!" denied Searle. "I wasn't sleepy, after all, so I was going back to the bar!"

"Without me?" he asked in a tone that sent shivers rippling through her. The searing glitter in his eyes as he looked her up and down shook the breath from her. She took a step back, unable to bear the heat of the naked passion in that look.

Taking her step back for an invitation, Buck entered, then shut the door and plunged the bolt into place.

Searle watched him wide-eyed, her breath coming in short, quick gasps. She thought she would be unable to breathe at all when he slowly faced her to let his gaze rest on the sloping neckline of her dress, which exposed the soft white swell of her breasts. His hands stole up under the caped top to lightly caress her bare arms. Searle trembled.

"Lord, you feel warm and inviting," he murmured, his voice a bare rustle of sound. One hand trailed gently over her, following the soft edge of her bodice, grazing her skin until Searle thought she would faint with the torment of her need. Feeling as if she were in someone else's body, she slid against him, a low guttural moan escaping her lips.

Instantly, Buck's lips and hands were in her hair, on her throat, over her cheeks, kissing and touching with punishing brevity. The impassioned plea that came from Searle startled her. His hand was at her back, tugging the zipper down its track. She did not care, she only cared about the flicker of his tongue upon her hungry lips. Buck pushed the clingy material away from her shoulders, down over her hips, until the dress fell like a pool of lilac at his feet.

With a soft oath, he gathered her into his arms and stretched her across the bed. As he imprisoned her there with his hard length, she felt the shudders that ran through his muscles and knew a moment of feminine triumph. With a swift urgency, his hands worked to remove the last of her clothes, flinging her lacy underwear into the air without taking his eyes from her. For one instant he was still, his breath sharply drawn, and then his hands were greedily exploring her every curve, every hollow, as if his touch would devour the beauty of her nakedness.

He strung a ribbon of kisses down the length of her throat, over the slope of her shoulders and across the fullness of her breasts, sending endless cascades of pleasure through her until Searle could no longer bear not touching him. Feverishly, vibrating with the need to experience the feel of him against her, she began yanking at the buttons on his shirt, until she popped one off in her haste. Pressing her palms and then her lips against his bared chest, she thrilled to the groan wrenched from deep within him. She arched upward, pushing aside the fabric of his shirt to imprint his taut muscles with her enticing curves.

Breathing heavily, he shifted his weight slightly away from her. "Tell me you want me, Searle," commanded Buck gruffly into the silk of her hair fanned across the bed.

"I want you, Buck, I want you," she sighed obediently. Twining her hands into the thickness of his golden hair, she drew his lips back down to hers, teasing him with darting nips.

He pulled gently away again. "Tell me you need me," he ordered in a voice thick with need.

"Please, Buck," begged Searle on a near groan.

"Tell me, Searle!"

"I need you, I need you, I need you," she whispered against the edge of his lips, her tongue punctuating every breathy pause.

A raspy moan dragged from Buck as he captured the fullness of her lips, parting them, tasting the sweetness within. Her hands sketched over the muscles of his back, drawing a quiver of response that shook them both. He moaned again. "Tell me you love me."

She answered him with fierce, hungry kisses that roamed his lips, his cheeks, his neck. Those were words she could not say and she tried to drown his demand in the swirling whirlpool of her passion. But he brought his loving mouth up to her ear, warm wisps of his breath stirring her hair as he murmured, "Tell me, tell me you love me."

Her legs tangled over his, her arms encircled his neck as Searle buried her face into the taut muscles of his shoulder. She heard him sigh deeply, felt him nuzzle the smoothness of her cheek. She raised her head to meet his kiss, a kiss almost without passion. Through her delirium, Searle thought the taste of his lips both sweet and sad. After a lingered withdrawal, Buck lifted his lips from hers and rolled away to sit up. Searle's eyes, glazed with passion, opened wide to gaze at him with bewilderment.

"What—what are you doing?" she asked as she watched him slowly rebutton his shirt. His chest heaved with each deep breath he forced himself to take and Searle saw his body convulse as he strove for control. With the last button in place, he leaned over her, cupping her face between his large hands.

"Searle, listen to me. I want you as I have never before wanted any woman. I want you so much the need is driving me mad. But a roll in the hay isn't going to satisfy me. I thought it would, I hoped it would, but it won't."

"I want you, Buck," breathed Searle, her voice filled with impassioned desire.

"Oh, God." His palms pressed into the bones of her cheek. She saw his chest rise and fall heavily. "For me, Searle, the wanting and the loving are the same thing. My need for you goes beyond the bed. That means—damn you!—more than a steamy night in a hotel room. That means I want you committed to me in every way."

Searle closed her eyes to shut out the sight of him lacerating her with his razor gaze. How could he be doing this to her? She needed him! She would go mad with her need of him! And he was demanding what she could not give. Frustration and fear came together in anger. "Are you saying you loved all the others?"

"No!" he admitted harshly. "I'm saying I love you. With the others, the bed satisfied me; with you, it won't. And I won't let you use me."

Abruptly, his hands dropped from her face. Opening her eyes, Searle reached out and clutched his arm to keep him from rising. "Buck, don't go, please," she ardently begged. "I'm not using you—"

"Yes, you were!" he cut in with a slash. "You were going to use me to release your own physical needs and to hell with what I might be needing from you! What I felt never touched you, nothing ever touches you!"

"That's not true!" she denied on a desperate whisper. "You touch me—"

His sharp intake of breath silenced her. He released the breath on a long drawn-out sigh and stood. "Don't you know what you're doing to me?" he demanded, his voice curiously gentle. "Deep down inside, there's a warm, vibrant woman in you, a woman worth loving, but you keep that part of you locked up within some kind of frozen cell. That's the woman I want, Searle. But how can I get through to her if I don't know what I'm up against? Tell me, for God's sake, tell me and we'll work it out together!"

How could she tell him? What could she say that he would possibly understand? Dredging up the bitter memories wouldn't bring emotional security to Searle. She knew she had taken a step toward it, toward him, with her physical need for him, but Buck wanted her to leap a gap as dangerously wide as the Grand Canyon, and she knew she was not ready to jump.

Each attempt to breathe became a painful gasp of air, each beat of her heart an aching blow. She met his eyes and he saw the refusal in the emerald crystal of hers. Slowly, Buck dropped his eyes to run over her naked length. Instinctively, Searle crossed her hands over her breasts to shield herself from the cruelty of his stare. The grim glint of his eyes mercilessly flicked over her like a painful, stinging whip. She wanted to strike out at him, hurt him as his quiet words and hard look were hurting her, but her tongue felt leaden and she suffered silently.

His fingertip reached out and lightly stroked the planes of her cheek. "You're so damned lovely," he said roughly. "But I want a commitment of more than your lovely body. I'd even be willing to settle for a live-in arrangement, but I suspect you'd want a cold, lifeless affair, forcing me to sneak in and out of your arms like some damn thief in the night." He saw by the sudden wild flaring of her nostrils that he was right and he said harshly, "Well, dammit, I'm not a thief! I don't want to take love, I want to be given it!"

Searle turned her face away so that his hand brushed the soft spray of her hair. With ragged breaths, she mumbled, "I was about to give it—"

"No, you damn well weren't!" snapped Buck. Gripping her chin tightly, he forced her to face him, then tapped her forehead with his finger. "Love comes from here and"—tapping the swell of her breasts—"here. What you were giving had nothing to do with love because you weren't using your heart and soul, only this."

He crushed his lips fiercely into hers in a taking that was not a kiss, but a punishment. One hand twisted into her hair, tugging in a deliberate effort to hurt, while the other hand roughly enfolded the softness of her breast.

No longer warm, no longer hungry for him, Searle

struggled wildly against the brutality of his assault, but his strength pinned her helplessly to the bed. With sudden swiftness, he let her go, standing again and staring down at her body.

"Get out!" she spat at him, sitting upright. "Get out!"

"An hour from now, I'm going to call myself a fool," he muttered, turning away. But he halted and whirled to face her once more. "Call me when you're ready to come out of that shell of yours, Searle. Call me when you're ready for love."

"Don't hold your breath waiting," she hissed. "I have all I want out of life. I have my career, my independence. I don't need love. And I certainly don't need you!"

Though he shrugged before he left, Searle knew she'd hurt him by the dark flare in his eyes. She was glad. She wanted him to hurt, to feel as anguished as she. He'd charmed her into offering what she'd never given—her desire, her need for him, but he'd cast it back at her with words that flayed her soul. That was the bitter irony, the supreme jest! Buck had said her heart and soul weren't there for him, but they were, they were, and it was only as the door clicked shut that Searle had known this.

So this was love, she thought dully. This biting torment that threatened to strip her soul raw. This was worse, much worse, than she'd ever imagined. Hugging her slim, naked frame, Searle swayed sideways on the bed, telling herself the ache would go away. Must go away.

Oh, dear Lord, if she ran after Buck, told him she was ready to love, did love him, what then? How much happiness would she gain against how much grief?

Inevitably, disillusionment would come and Searle knew she'd never endure it. This way, she was safe. Eventually, the piercing pain would cease and she'd return to the safety of her job, her apartment, her life as it was before Buck had shattered her shell. She would glue the shards back together and go on, knowing she was safe from further, worse misery.

Sometime later—she did not know how much later—she got up, crawled into her pajamas and under the covers. But she did not sleep. She lay awake, aching with a feverish desire that horrified her. Listening to the steadily drumming rain as it muted the blare from the streets below, she promised herself never again, never again would she subject herself to this torment.

CHAPTER TWELVE

In the weeks that followed her trip to New York, Searle threw herself into the safety of never-ending work. She took over assignments for the newspapers as well as the magazine and often brought home pieces to work on late into the night. For as long as she could, she had lingered over the Carlton feature, as if through each word she somehow touched the man. But at last she finished it, handing it in to Lenn with a tight smile that conveyed nothing of the wrenching heartache she felt. For her, it was the symbolic finish of their brief, unsettling relationship.

The feature was the best thing she'd ever written. Entitled "Baseball's Golden Boy with the Midas Touch," it vividly brought out the warmth and color of Buck Carlton's vibrant personality. A detailed portrait painted in words, the feature was, quite simply, good. Lenn wanted to enter it for an award from a regional magazine association, but Searle refused to allow this. She wanted it over and done with. She wanted the whole episode out of her mind.

But the episode would not easily be banished from her thoughts. Little things constantly conjured up memories of Buck, always affecting her deeply. Once when she took some copy directly down to typesetting, she heard the low rumble of the presses in the room beyond and was vividly reminded of Buck's laughter. Such incidents disturbed her long after she gave up hope of ever being with Buck again.

The week after she returned from New York, a persistent flame of hope flickered unbidden within her. But when the Blues ended their road trip and she heard nothing from Buck for the six agonizing days of their next home stand, the flame died out. During that time, she'd fought against a constant urge to call him. Once she had actually had the phone in her hand, but pride kept her from dialing. She wouldn't give Buck Carlton such a victory.

Gradually, Searle came to accept his rejection, and with acceptance came a denial that she had ever loved him at all. As she had once told Buck, the very idea was ludicrous. She congratulated herself on preventing future, worse misery, then with the next breath, wondered how any misery could be worse than what she now felt. Of course, she never answered that. She continued to tell herself the constant, dull ache would soon go away.

A small change crept into her daily pattern. It began with the sports page. She found herself reading it thoroughly first thing every morning, as though donning some hair shirt in penance for having imagined herself to be in love. One night she carried her clock radio into the living room and listened to the Blues' game broadcast. After that, it became a regular routine. Thus, she knew Buck continued his outstanding hitting and fielding, and while a part of her felt inexplicably proud of him, most of her experienced a surge of bitter anger. Obviously, the loss of her had not affected him in the slightest degree. How much, she asked herself sharply, could he have really loved her?

One Sunday in mid-August, Searle escaped the emptiness of her apartment by listlessly wandering through a shopping mall. She noticed a knot of men gathered around a television display and joined the circle in time to see a close-up of Buck Carlton, grinning easily and confidently as he poised, muscles taut, ready to bat. Her heart gave a wrenching leap and she ignored the voice that told her to walk away. A high fly ball put Buck out and Searle left the group of men to approach a salesman.

She returned home with a portable color set, which she

ridiculously refused, at first, to turn on. But eventually, Searle began to watch every televised game. It was like self-flagellation, a punishment she meted out to herself along with the hair shirt of the sports stories; a punishment for her failure to guard against being hurt, for allowing herself to imagine even briefly that she loved Buck Carlton. Or was it hate that she had felt?

Love and hate. Hadn't she realized long ago that they were merely different shades of the same color, both capable of darkening the soul? She had mistaken her feelings that night for the softer emotion simply by virtue of her physical needs. But actually, she now believed, she had hated him all along—hated him for disrupting the peaceful, sensible pattern of her life in a way that seemed irreparable.

And he, of course, had resented the fact that unlike all the women in a long line before her, she had not fallen at his feet avowing her devotion. Buck was a man used to winning. His pique at not winning her had been obvious, but it still stunned Searle to recall the way he had coldly turned off his passionate drive just to punish her. He had brutally meant to pay her back for her refusal to tell him what he wanted to hear. For that, too, she hated him.

She watched him and read about him with, she told herself, a purely academic interest in discovering what it had been about him that he of all men had managed to cause her such pain.

Over the weeks, the body that had been slim became thin. The curves lost their allure. The angular face became gauntly chiseled. Searle's beauty began to fade like that of a wilting flower's, but she didn't see any of her reflection beyond the sorrow in her eyes. Had she noticed her looks, she would not have cared.

Then one day, Lenn called her into his office. First he coughed, then he shuffled papers, and at last he got to the point.

"I'm giving you the next two weeks off," he said bluntly.

Startled, Searle turned her head from the view out his window. "What?"

"You're to take the next two weeks off. Paid."

"But—but I don't want them off," she stammered.

Lenn took off his glasses, stared at them against the light, then slowly readjusted them upon his nose. "I don't know what's wrong, Searle, but I do know you've lost weight, lost color. I've noticed all the work you've put in on the papers as well as *Our Town.* If overwork's the problem, then I'm taking care of it."

"Don't be ridiculous," she said with a hint of her old snap. "You know I can handle the work. I'm not overworked."

"You obviously need rest. Look in a mirror!" suggested Roberts gruffly. "The rings under your eyes have become permanent fixtures! I won't have it said I'm working you to death," he added in an attempt at lightness.

"But I've had my vacation time for the year. I took it last April, remember?" she said. Her voice nearly broke. She didn't need any more time with nothing to fill it but thoughts of Buck. Such thoughts were driving her mad anyway.

"Consider this a bonus. For the superb job you did on that Carlton feature," said Lenn. "That story's the best you've—"

She flinched as if struck. "Please, Lenn, I really don't want to take time off. I'll quit the extra hours and get more rest, I promise." She sounded like a child promising to be good. Roberts's brows nearly reached his receding gray hairline, but he didn't ask the question ringing through his mind.

"Well, if you're sure," he began hesitantly.

"Oh, I am, really I am. I wouldn't know what to do with myself if you gave me two weeks off," she said truthfully.

She tried an offhand laugh that came out brittle. "I'm married to my job, you know."

"Well, at least take the rest of the day off—tomorrow, too," insisted Roberts, leaning across the clutter on his desk to stab a finger at her. "Take the weekend to relax. And if you don't start looking better, young lady, I'll personally haul you off to my doctor to find out what's wrong with you!"

The paternal threat brought forth one of her rare smiles. "All right, boss. Anything you say."

But when she left his office, Searle was shaking. She went straight to the ladies' room and stared hard at the thin, gaunt, melancholy creature reflected beneath the garish light. Lord, it was true. She looked like a scarecrow someone had hung a hank of hair onto. She unrolled her hair and stared harder. No improvement. Oh, well, she thought with a shrug, at least men aren't panting at my heels anymore. But Searle didn't put her hair back up and she casually stopped by Norman Kraekor's desk on her way home.

Norm's desk held the end position of a long row of desks filled with ad copy, order sheets, and identical telephones constantly in use. The low rumble of many voices speaking into phones and the muted scratch of pens crossing paper provided the backdrop to her nervousness as Searle waited patiently for Norm to end his call.

When she had first returned from New York, Searle had been so coldly disdainful of her fellow workers that even Norm had stopped coming by her office. Without realizing it, she had missed the contact and she knew now she'd always felt guilty about her treatment of him. Whatever his motivations, Norm had always been kind to her and she had no right to take out her aggressions on him. He hung up and looked at her now in surprise, then smiled the toothy grin.

"Hiya, doll!" he said. Then the smile faded and he

added in quick concern, "Have you been sick or something?"

"Oh, just a bit run down, Norm. I'm being sent home for a couple of days to recuperate. Lenn told me if I didn't look better soon, they'd be blaming him for my demise." She smiled and even in the wan face it was a seductive smile. Norm immediately grinned and ogled her with his colorless eyes.

"Yeah, well, I'd heard you'd been carrying quite a load," he said. He stood up and came around the metal desk to stand beside her. "How's about I walk you to your car? You look pretty weak, like a kitten."

She didn't protest, letting him take her elbow with unaccustomed familiarity and pace with her out to the parking lot. She asked him how he'd been and he talked to her with his usual air of self-importance. As she withdrew her keys from her purse and turned to unlock her car, he broke off and said, "Look, honey, I've got these tickets to a dinner-dance next week. It's a charity benefit and, well, babe, I thought maybe you'd like to go." He said it rather uncertainly, as if he weren't sure he should ask her.

"Oh, I—" She paused. Why not? Did she want to sit home alone every night of her life? "I'd really like to, Norman. Eating is just what Lenn prescribed for me. When did you say?"

"Hey, that's great, baby, just great!" said Norm with enthusiasm. "The dinner is a week from Saturday night. Like I said, it's a charity deal and in my line of work, it's one of those have-to functions, but with you there, honey, work will definitely become a pleasure."

"Fine. I'll see you on Monday," she said, slipping into her car and firmly closing the door. She'd probably regret her decision all the weeks to come when Norm would be hanging around her office all the time, but right now she was happy she'd said yes. And now she had three and a half big days to fill without leaving any room for dangerous thinking.

Surprisingly, it turned out to be less of a chore than she had anticipated. Having heard that sparkling wine will often work as a sedative, she stopped on her way home and purchased a bottle of Asti Spumante. Each night, she drank a glass before retiring and slept better than she had in weeks. She also made herself eat more than an occasional nibble and found herself relaxing in the summer sun by the apartment pool on Sunday morning, feeling better and congratulating herself on coming out of the doldrums at last.

She soaked in the morning sun for nearly an hour before deciding she didn't wish to be burned to a crisp. Grabbing her morning paper from the hallway as she entered her apartment, she read it over brunch. She ate a light salad as she finished the front-page news, then turned automatically to the sports section. She pulled it out, then froze, the sheet of paper hanging limply from her hand. With a jerk, she spread it on her countertop and stared.

There was a picture of Buck—a disheveled, frowning Buck, his arm draped possessively over a voluptuous blonde. The headline screamed at her. "Mr. Aggressive Swings Again." Then, below that, the teaser read, "Hard-hitting Slugger Levels Fan."

Quickly, she scanned the article. "Buck Carlton, All-Star right fielder for the Blues, proved his ability to swing off the field as well as on in a brawl in a Chicago bar late last night. Carlton decked Henry Rogers, a reported baseball fan, after Rogers made what witnesses claimed to be disparaging remarks about Carlton's companion, Miss Susie Winslow. None of the parties involved were available for comment.

"Earlier, Carlton continued in his outstanding display of . . ." Searle's eyes blurred, and she dropped the paper. Brawling! Over a woman! It made her feel sick, absolutely ill. Getting a grip on herself, she very slowly picked up the paper and stared at the photo again. Well, he hadn't wasted any time in finding a replacement for her. But then, it was what she'd expected, and there was no reason at all for her to feel this oppressive pressure that made it painful for her to breathe.

Was this how her mother always felt? wondered Searle fleetingly. No wonder she had been so bitter, so hateful. Not, of course, that what Searle felt could be as strong as the consuming jealousy of her mother. It was more like relief, she told herself.

She carefully folded the paper together, then dumped it all in the trash. She did not mean to let this destroy the equilibrium she'd struggled so hard to regain. It made her furious with herself for allowing the photo and story to upset her even momentarily, and even more so for permitting Buck to still give her the least pain. It was over, completely and finally over, and she did not want it to be otherwise.

Through the week, she continued the routine of the glass of wine at night and soaking in the late afternoon sun, so that she began to regain her natural beauty. The deep shadows faded from under her emerald eyes and the bronze tint from the sun added a healthy glow to her smooth skin. Though she still looked far too thin, she managed to gain a little weight and with it the confidence that she would be looking very good when Norman arrived to collect her on Saturday evening.

She chose a fitted white sundress to show off her new tan and complemented the simplicity of her dress with a drop of pink coral hung on a white-gold chain. Wanting very much to have an evening of fun, she'd taken her time over applying her makeup and brushing her hair until she knew she looked better than she had in weeks. The lustrous mane of her hair fell softly against her bare shoulders and gave her the feeling of a cool assurance.

The effort did not go to waste. Norman's thin, swarthy cheeks puffed out, then caved in when she let him into her apartment.

"Wow!" he stated, forgetting to grin. "You're gonna knock 'em all dead, honey! You look tee-riff-ic!" Then he remembered his polished smile and Searle returned the compliment.

"You look fine yourself, Norm." She was relieved to see a pair of khaki slacks had replaced his usual polyester-knit and an open collar lime green sport shirt was tucked neatly into them. Beyond telling her that the benefit was a casual affair, Norm had not given her any details about the evening ahead, and as she handed him a gin and tonic, she asked, "What is this dinner a benefit for?"

"The Crippled Children's Hospital," he answered, eyeing her steadily over his drink. *Tonight,* he was thinking, *might just be my lucky night.* She'd never treated him so warmly and that dress was strictly meant to turn a guy on. It did, too. "Half the price of every ticket sold will go directly to the hospital, the other half to pay the expenses at Martoni's. Hope you like pasta, doll."

"Oh, I do, especially when it's good," she replied with a smile. "The Italian cuisine at Martoni's is excellent."

"Yeah," he agreed. "And the gimmick for this thing is pretty smart, too. Did I tell you about it, babe?"

"No. What kind of gimmick do you mean?" she asked absently. She was glancing at her watch, trying to determine just when they should leave. The way Norm was ogling her over his drink, it was obvious that the less amount of time spent alone, the better. She wanted a fun evening out, but she didn't want to be dodging his advances more often than she had to.

"Well, all the waiters and bartenders and busboys and help will be local celebrities—you know, TV newsmen, radio deejays, sports figures . . ."

Her head came up at that. "Sports figures?" she echoed,

her heart beginning to falter in its beat.

"Sure, doll. You know, jocks," laughed Norm. "They haven't announced who all was to be there, but all the pro teams—football, basketball, and baseball—will be represented."

"Do you"—she licked her lips in a way that severely disrupted Norm's thought processes—"do you know if—which Blues' players will be there?"

"Nope," he answered, downing the end of his drink at a gulp. He didn't notice the sudden frantic gleam in her eyes, nor the furrow in her brow. He only noticed the tantalizing way the tawny hint of her breast rose and fell above the edge of her white sundress. "But don't you worry, babe, I'll keep all the jocks away from you."

There didn't seem to be any way she could get out of this. Norm was already standing, looking at her questioningly. Perhaps, she prayed as she stood, perhaps he wouldn't be there. Perhaps this would be one charity event he wouldn't be in on.

"The ballplayers will be celebrating tonight, anyway. They took another victory this afternoon," said Norman as he escorted her to his sporty car. "That team can't seem to lose this year—I'm putting down money they go all the way to the Big One this season."

"Really?" said Searle, with enough frost to define clearly her lack of interest.

Remembering that she disliked the subject of sports, Norman immediately switched to shoptalk, a subject that managed to ease the guarded set to her lovely mouth by the time they reached the restaurant.

Martoni's Italian Gardens had an old-world charm that for once failed to beguile Searle. Her eyes darted obliquely about the spacious, table-filled room, searching the faces among the laughing, chattering crowds. Straw-covered wine bottles and baskets hung against brick walls and dangled randomly from the beamed ceiling, adding to the cheerful atmosphere instilled by the red-and-white checked cloths splashed over the tables. Everywhere the blinding flash of camera lights spoke of the media presence, while occasionally a brilliant light would illuminate a patch in the shadows and a man shouldering a heavy rectangular camera would film a moment of action for television.

Searle saw all this, but she did not see Buck Carlton. Joking lightly with their waiter, a local TV weatherman she'd instantly recognized, she began to relax. She continued to cast surreptitious glances about the restaurant throughout the meal, paying little actual attention to either her lasagna or Norm's conversation. By meal's end, her inner quaking ceased. Though she'd spotted a number of Blues' players, the All-Star right fielder had not been among them. For once, it appeared she was going to be lucky.

One square section of wooden floor had been cleared of tables and shortly after eight a rock band took its place at the far end of the room. The crowded bar was on the other end of the small dance floor and as the evening wore on, more and more people seemed to gravitate in that direction. Norman watched the activity with a barely suppressed enthusiasm. He always wanted to be where the action was; he looked from the bar to Searle.

"What d'you say, honey?" he asked, leaning as close as possible to her. "How's about a drink or a dance? Or both?"

She didn't necessarily want to be in Norman's clutches on the dance floor, but she had promised herself to make the evening fun for them both. With a slight nod, she agreed and found herself being led through the congested dining area onto the dimly lit cleared patch. There, the press of bodies forced her closer into Norm's arms than she would have liked and Searle began to wish she'd worn a dress with a higher cut to the back. His hands seemed determined to explore as much of her bared skin as possible, causing her to realize that the evening would have to end much sooner than she'd originally planned. As soon as the number ended, Searle broke from his clasp and smiled.

"How about that drink now, Norm?" she queried.

"Ah, honey, I thought another dance—" he began, not taking his eyes off the squared neckline of her dress.

"I really could use that drink," she said firmly. "It's so warm in here with all the crush of people. I'd like something cool—a daiquiri."

"Okay, babe. We can dance again later," he said, rubbing his hand along her arm as he pulled her toward the bar.

That's what you think, she mentally denied. No way was she going to let herself in for more of his clumsy pawing. This drink and then home, she decided.

Throngs of people overflowed the area around the bar. Standing her at the edge of the crowd, Norm promised to return with the drinks as soon as he could, then disappeared into the swarm. For one instant, Searle considered ducking out and grabbing a cab home, but she realized how absolutely unfair this would be to Norm and reluctantly decided to stick it out. She'd just have to freeze his advances later, that's all.

She became absorbed in watching the swaying of bodies as people moved in the sleepy swirl of a slow dance. Her body unconsciously joined the rhythm, swaying slightly. She liked to dance; if only Norm could keep his hands to himself. Maybe when he got back they could try it again. . . . Suddenly, a firm hand captured the flesh of her arm, jolting her out of her reverie.

"Oh, Norm," began Searle, turning. She stopped, her breath torn from her throat with wrenching pain. Her heart twisted, stemming her life's blood until she turned ghostly pale beneath her tan.

CHAPTER THIRTEEN

"Care to dance?" asked Buck, already propelling her into the flow of dancers.

Her first moment of shock was followed instantly by a plummeting of her heart. Though Buck was smiling at her, it was nothing more than a small, tight lift of the corners of his mouth, never reaching his eyes. His lids were lowered, but Searle could see the angry contempt stabbing at her from the dark eyes. She halted, tried to resist the force of his hand on her arm.

"No, thank you!" she rasped, attempting to wrench free.

Wordlessly, Buck yanked her into the circle of his arms, compelling her to match the fluid motion of his body. He easily clamped her arms down, then crushed her further resistance with his hands compressed snugly upon her spine. She stayed stiff and tense within his hold, trying not to respond to the magnetic closeness of him. She had fallen under his spell once and suffered greatly; she did not intend to be so foolish again.

Through her thin sundress, she could feel the hard muscles of his chest ripple as he slowly steered them into the center of the dancers, and she felt the unwanted desire flare to life within her. It would not be denied. She unconsciously tilted toward him and, with a real smile, Buck loosened the tension of his grip.

"My—my date," protested Searle with a feeble breath, still trying to retain her sanity.

"Surely he can spare you for one dance," said Buck shortly.

They moved without speaking, body pressed close to body, each breath exchanging warmth. His hands fondled her sensitive skin with a measured deliberation that had her wishing the music would never stop. As if of their own accord, her arms stretched upward to encircle his neck and her fingers gently played with the short rough hairs on his nape.

As the music faded away, they stood motionless, clinging to each other wordlessly. Then, as a blast of rock and roll galvanized the people around them, Buck grasped Searle's wrist and pulled her through the crowd. He passed behind the band and down a corridor into a small, smoke-filled room with dingy aqua-green walls endlessly multiplied by a long mirror spread across one wall. Half-filled glasses and discarded cigarettes sat beside overflowing ashtrays on a ledge that ran the length of the mirror. Empty instrument cases were strewn about the floor and jackets were flung over the room's few chairs.

No sooner had Buck closed the door when Searle strode toward it, reaching for the knob. His hand deflected hers before he moved to block the doorway, arms crossed over his chest. In this garish light, she saw that he wore a bartender's red garter on the long sleeve of a frilled white shirt that was tucked carelessly into a pair of tight, faded jeans. She refused to look up beyond the middle of the shirt.

"What are you doing?" she demanded, each word a breathy staccato. "I have to get back. Norman will be looking for me."

"Let him look. We have to talk."

She looked up then and saw that the anger in Buck's eyes had been replaced by a glittering shaft of light that sent her senses reeling.

"Talk about what?" she inquired in a voice devoid of the staggering emotion she felt. The dance had assaulted her senses; she could not deny the ecstatic pleasure she had felt when she was in his arms. But Searle was warier now, determined to overcome her weakness. New York had taught her a lesson she wasn't about to forget. "I thought we had already done all our talking."

He leaned against the wood of the door, running his eyes restlessly over her. Though the stance was casual, the look was not, and Searle felt heated color rush over her cheeks as his eyes lingered on the exposed swell of her breasts. The uncertainty that attacked her whenever he was near her struck again and she felt her reserve melting away. She feared her loss of control, she knew how much he could hurt her, yet she didn't seem able to stop it.

"What are you doing here tonight?" he asked on a note of demand.

"I came because Norman brought me," she replied tersely. She wasn't going to let him see how he was undermining her emotional stability.

"What are you trying to do—make me jealous?" inquired Buck coldly, his eyes shuttered. "You can forget it. No matter how I feel about you seeing this guy, I have no right to get jealous. That right comes when my ring's on your finger."

"I'm doing no such thing!" she denied. She felt the color flood her cheeks again, but knew this time it was from anger. "I wouldn't *want* to make you jealous if I could."

"No? Then what are you doing here with that jerk? And don't try to tell me it's because you've got something going with him. I don't believe it." His voice was taunting, derisive.

"I'm not asking you to believe anything," she returned. With a deep breath, her eyes fixed firmly on the elastic red slash on his sleeve, she added, "I'm out with Norm because he's my friend. Or is that the sort of relationship you don't understand?"

"You're a big girl, Searle, and if you want to play these games, it's your choice, not mine," said Buck, a mocking note in his voice. "But it's strictly solitaire, lady. I'm not playing."

She turned away, not wanting him to see her inner struggle with her own weakness. Tossing two jackets from a chair to the floor, she sat, folding her hands in her lap, and calmly asked, "Is that all you wished to discuss, or is there more?"

"You still haven't told me why you're here," he said. He left the door and came toward her, her heart pounding harder with each step. When he reached her chair, he bent, collecting a strand of her hair and teasing it through his fingers. "If not to make me jealous, then why? That dress is damned provocative, Searle—"

"You don't seriously believe that was for you, do you?" she snapped. His touch was destroying her rationality, making her weak with her need for him. She retreated to the protection of anger. Knocking his hand from her hair, she hotly declared, "God, I knew you super-jocks had massive egos but this surpasses all belief! I dressed to please my date and no one else. I didn't even know where he was taking me," she added half-truthfully, "but if I'd known you were to be here, believe me, I'd have worn a suit of armor!"

She tried to jump up, but he threw his hands against her shoulder and pressed her down into the chair. "Just wanted you to know, lady, that you scored a big fat zip with this game. You can't make me believe you dressed like this"—his fingers played above the neckline of her sundress, branding her skin with his touch—"to please that jerk who thinks he's Mr. Cool."

She thrust his hands away and leaped to her feet. "I really am not interested in what you believe, Buck Carlton!" she announced with heat. "If you want to think I'd care what you thought, that's your problem. Now, if you'll excuse me, my date will be looking for me."

She was secretly surprised when he made no effort to stop her from striding to the door, and she threaded her way through the bodies undulating across the floor with a sense of disappointment. She found Norman back at their table, looking bewildered and disgusted.

"Oh, there you are," he said, trying not to sound exasperated. "I've been looking all over for you."

"Sorry. I had to repair the hem of my dress—it had come down somehow." She smiled apologetically, then took a gulp of her daiquiri. Two more gulps and the drink had vanished. She heard the strains of a soft ballad beginning and thrust her lip out at Norman. "You did say we'd dance again, didn't you?"

"Sure, babe, sure," he agreed rapidly. Pushing aside the remainder of his drink, he practically dashed to gather her into his arms.

Maneuvering him easily, Searle soon had them at the edge of the dance floor, near the bar. She entwined herself against him, resting her head on his shoulder. As Norm was jubilantly thinking this was indeed his lucky night, she studied the men behind the bar from beneath lowered lashes. With an intake of breath that caused Norm to nuzzle her cheek, she saw Buck watching them through narrowed eyes. He was grinning, but his grin was belied by the forceful slam onto the bar of each glass he filled.

The idea of making Buck jealous grew to be a need within her. If he wanted to think she'd play at such games, well, he'd get what he wanted. A streak of pleasure in her power to wound him underscored her desire to hit out at him in this age-old manner. She snuggled closer to Norman, but felt her sense of triumph dissolve as his hands dipped beneath the low edge of her dress at her back.

"Please, Norm," she said dampingly as she squirmed away from his touch.

"Ah, babe, you want it, you know you do," he mumbled into her ear. His breath felt moist, sticky. "Let's say we ditch this joint, honey, and get down to some real good times."

Her head jerked up, and she tried to push out of his

grasp. At that same instant, Norman's arms left her so abruptly that she staggered to keep her balance. She heard a tremendous whack that seemed to reverberate through all the music and noise, then she saw Norm lying amidst a tangle of feet on the floor, with Buck towering over him. Flashbulbs began to burst, and the next thing she knew, she was being dragged from the scene while Buck thrust microphones and cameras from their path.

The first wave of humid, hot night air seemed refreshing after the close, smoky fog inside the restaurant, but the air quickly became oppressive. She tried to pull her wrist free, but received a jerk that jangled her nerve endings up to her teeth. Buck shoved her into the leather seat of his BMW, then slammed the door shut on her, all without saying a word. As he got into his side, a babble of voices and a number of faceless cameras and lights swarmed over the car, but he plunged into gear and left them behind with a roar.

"Tell me," bit out Searle in a release of nervous tension, "do you intend to make brawling a weekly habit?"

Suddenly, unexpectedly, Buck grinned. Running one hand through his hair, he said with a laugh, "Damn you, Searle—I'm going to get slapped one hell of a fine for this. I just hope I don't get suspended as well. It could screw up my chances for the record."

She stared at him in stunned silence. He looked as if he'd just been wreathed with the laurels of victory. She felt the rage heating up within her until it exploded fiercely. "I don't believe this! You make a scene worthy of some grade-C movie, subjecting me to God knows how many photos and stories to come, and all you can worry about is your damned record! Well, for your information, I'm no Susie Winslow"—she sneered the name—"thrilled to be the reason for your latest brawl! You can just stop this car and let me out now."

"Well, I'm sorry," he began on a rising note of anger.

"Sorry! I should say so!" she cut in. "What about Norman? You should be apologizing to him, for God's sake!"

"I'm not sorry about that," said Buck through his teeth. "I hope I broke his lousy jaw."

"Well, I hope he sues you!" she retorted. "And I asked to be let out!"

"I'm not letting you out. We have things to discuss."

"Oh? I thought we already had all that settled," said Searle acidly. "Only it looks like you were wrong—you acted like a jealous, lovesick idiot back there. And after all that talk about rights."

He shot her a sideways glance, then shifted gears with an angry spurt. "That's just the point. I have no right to feel the way I do, but I admit it—I wanted to kill that bastard. I saw him pawing you out there and I wanted to—"

"What was your reason last week?" she interrupted, her voice cold and clear. She couldn't forget the image of the news photo she'd seen. The vision made her long to hurt him as much as possible. "Did that poor man paw Susie, too? Or was hitting him just one of those things you fun-loving jocks get your jollies on? I thought you said you were an even-tempered guy," she ended sarcastically.

"I used to be, before I met you! But you've got me so messed up, I'm lucky to have any kind of temper left to me at all," he clipped back through clenched teeth. The large hands tightly gripping the steering wheel gleamed white in the darkness.

"Oh, you have a temper all right," she threw out. "A foul one!"

"You knew what you were doing tonight! God, I could have strangled you for egging me on!"

He wheeled the car into her parking lot with a screech that slashed through the heat of their argument. Within moments, Buck was marching her up to her apartment like a guard with his prisoner. Beneath the glare of resentment she shot at him lay a glitter of repressed excitement. A secret, utterly feminine thrill over his dramatic display of jealousy heightened the sexual tension she felt. If only there had been no condemning picture of Susie Winslow, Searle might have thrown away all caution, all resistance, and fallen straight into his arms. But the bitter piercing image of his arm draped over the pretty blonde's shoulder had not dimmed; in fact, tonight's actions had only emphasized that peculiar memory. Anger flared anew at how easily he could hurt her.

When she flicked on her lights, Searle stepped rigidly into the center of the room, then whirled to face him. "Say what you have to say, then get out."

He stood gazing at her, his eyes hungry and darkly glowing, his hands shoved into the depths of his pockets. "If I had any sense, I'd get the hell out of here," he said brusquely. "But knowing you has robbed me of my sense, so I'm damn well staying until we've straightened things out."

Her heartbeat quickened. She had always thought it was his irresistible smile that cracked her defenses, but here he was scowling at her and she felt positively giddy. She looked away. She had just begun to get over the weeks of misery he'd caused—did she want to let him inflict more of the same all over again? With as much chill as her heated senses could muster, she said flatly, "I can't imagine what you think we have to discuss. These past few weeks have clearly shown the lack of anything between us."

"Oh, yes, the past few weeks!" he said raggedly. A bitter twist marred his face. "I've tried to fight this thing, tried to get over you. I told myself it was crazy—a woman like you would run me through the wringer. But when I saw you tonight, I knew it was all over but the signing." He grinned, a rueful smile shadowed by his moustache. "Hell,

I need you and I'm willing to take you on any terms. Your terms."

With a sharp intake of breath, she watched him lazily withdraw his hands from his pockets and move toward her. A frightened anticipation overwhelmed her. She had once thought a simple physical solution would settle things between them, but she doubted this now and the uncertainty lent a razor edge to her voice. "There are no terms. Whatever might have been between us ended in New York."

"Now there, lady, is where you're wrong," he said, the set of his jaw unyielding, the light of desire blatant in his eyes. "You may not be capable of loving me, but you'll respond to me, all right."

Fascinated, she watched the sensuous turn of his lips. She thought she should run, but she stood waiting, the physical tension almost unbearable.

"And now, Searle Delacorte," said Buck as he took her into his arms, "and now . . ."

He stilled her unspoken protests with lips that sweetly moistened hers, tenderly at first, then with a consuming urgency that startled her. Deft little flicks of his tongue over the full curve of her parted lips teased her senses into surrender. His hands roamed behind her, coursing over the smooth skin of her back, shattering Searle's consciousness into uncountable slivers of sensation. She moaned as his callused palm slid down to catch the metal of her zipper. There, he hesitated, half lifting his lips away from hers, as if he waited for her approval. She had no thought of stopping him, only of continuing the feel of his hands, his lips upon her heated body. Arching her head back, Searle took his mouth in an inflamed kiss that prompted his fingers to slide her zipper down.

Throwing her arms upward, she allowed him to tug the dress from her body, then reveled in the shuddering groan the sight of her naked breasts wrenched from him. For one long moment he seemed unable to move, and Searle thought she would die from the agony of her impatience. Suddenly Buck swept her up in one liquid motion, grasping her so tightly it hurt her to draw breath, then carried her into her bedroom. The room was as precise and colorless as he'd always imagined it would be, with one exception. A pink-and-white furry mouse leaned possessively over the top of her dresser. Seeing this, he stopped and laughed, a deep, throaty, satisfied laugh.

"You kept him," he said in a voice as tender as his touch. He laid her gently upon the bed, then quickly straightened to tear off his frilled shirt.

Breathlessly, Searle watched as the shirt fell from the powerful shoulders to the floor. His tautly muscled chest gleamed starkly in the muted light and the sinuous flexure of his rugged torso made her gasp with overwhelming need. The movement of his hands drew her eyes down to the narrow line of his hips, but as he began to unfasten the buckle of his leather belt, she hurriedly turned her face into the veil of her hair.

The bed gave soundlessly and she felt the warmth of his body as it moved against hers. He stroked the silky softness of her hair with one hand, while the other slid down to the cool, smooth satin of her cream briefs. His fingers skimmed over the fabric, then slowly slipped it down the length of her legs before returning swiftly to dally over the flat of her stomach. Beneath his touch, Searle trembled violently with a passionate excitement she'd never before known. He felt it and his breath came fast and hard.

Shifting his weight slightly away from her, Buck gazed at her for several long seconds. "Whatever you feel for me," he murmured thickly, "I want you to know that I love you, that I'm giving myself to you in love."

He gave her no chance to react to this, but feverishly claimed her lips in a series of fierce, clinging kisses that sent shudders of response rippling through her. As he bent his head to kiss the hollow of her throat, her hands pushed tightly into the golden thickness of his hair, then crossed wildly over his firm, round shoulders to press into the sinews of his back. His lips moved slowly down to nuzzle the drop of her necklace, which lay against her breastbone, and his hand delicately caressed her breast until Searle cried out with her explosive delight. Then Buck's thighs tangled with hers and their bodies blended together with the elemental naturalness of cloud with sky, light with shadow.

Sensations so sweet as to be almost unbearable burst through her as Buck rhythmically explored her innermost depths. She pressed her hands into the tensing muscles of his shoulders, thrilling as she felt them strain beneath her fingertips. Fire flowed through her bloodstream as his hands stroked the silken smoothness of her breasts; her skin burned with excitement where his heated breath grazed her neck. Searle's spirit kindled to life in the passionate conflagration of her senses, flaring beyond all reason, beyond anything she'd ever before known.

Afterward, Buck lay very still, with only his deep, unsteady draw of air to tell of his spent pleasure. Then he rolled over and circled Searle within the drowsy contentment of his arms. As they lay quietly together, she marveled at her feelings of fulfillment. For the first time, she had experienced the heights of passion and it completely blurred her assessment of herself. She no longer knew how far she could trust her own emotions.

Filled with doubt and wonder, she twisted her head to study Buck, only to find him watching her, propped on one elbow as his other arm draped possessively across her hip. There was no mistaking the triumphant glow of love in his eyes.

"I've never known it to be like this," he whispered, echoing her own thoughts.

Without warning, an image loomed before her and she

felt a stab of hostility. "I suppose that's what you said to Susie Winslow, too."

"Susie Wins—?" he began, puzzled, then his brow cleared and he laughed. Letting his fingers frisk lightly over her skin, he said, "I'm afraid not. I never even got into the batter's box with her."

Disbelief sketched over Searle's flushed face. "No?" She moistened her lips with her tongue in response to his capering touch and he quickly bent to kiss her.

"No," he replied as he lifted his lips from hers. "It's hard to get to bat when you call Susie 'Searle' while on deck." He chuckled against her mouth, sending pleasurable currents of warm breath across her lips. "I've never felt like this with any woman, Searle. It must be the love that adds the spice."

"You were quick to defend her honor," she pointed out in a husky tone. She turned her eyes to the cord of muscle along his arm. She didn't want to see that love in his eyes. It was too possessive and she didn't feel ready to admit anything beyond the physical gratification of their relationship. Anything more still hurt too much.

"Say, what is this? You jealous?" teased Buck, a hopeful note filling his voice.

"Don't be ridiculous!" she instantly denied. "I just wondered how much of tonight's little scene was due to chivalry and how much to habit."

He laughed lazily. "I wasn't defending anything before tonight. Susie Winslow was nothing but a baseball Annie—"

"A what?"

"A groupie," he explained. His hand continued to explore her body as if staking his claim, and Searle struggled to pay attention to what he was saying. "I picked her up—thought I could forget you for a while. But like I said, I didn't get too far. So we ended up in the bar, drinking.

When that idiot insulted her, I simply used it as an excuse to hit out at the world."

His hand moved to cup her breast, his thumb lightly bringing her nipple to a taut little peak. Searle tried to think, to ignore the resurgence of passion his teasing touch commanded over her. She wanted him, but she desperately needed time to think, to sort out all her conflicting emotions and understand what had really happened to her tonight. She forced her voice to work. "You—you did?"

His lopsided smile flashed. "I've wanted to plant my fist into something, someone, ever since New York. Frustration left me feeling nothing but angry inside. Until now." He brought his smile to her full lips, arousing her with the barest grazing. "You know how I feel now, Searle," he said in a voice slurred with desire. "Do you know yet how you feel?"

The gentle tone couldn't hide the tense ring coloring his question. Searle shied from it like a skittish colt. He said he loved her, but how long would that love last? How long before they began punishing each other for it? What they felt while kissing and touching had nothing to do with what they felt out of bed. Searle licked her lips, then raised her eyes to pass briefly over his.

"I—I wanted you," she admitted on a thread of a whisper.

Buck riveted her head onto the pillow with both hands pressed against her angular cheeks. "It's not a weakness to love someone, Searle," he stated flatly. "It's not a damned disease!"

Her tortured eyes told him she thought otherwise. Anger flashed through his brown eyes and he said in a voice tight with control, "Is that how you view it? Is that how you view me? Like some sickness you must get over?"

Again, he read the answer in her slanted eyes. Abruptly, he pulled his hands from her face, then he swung sideways to get up. She watched the shadow of him move through the darkened room as he gathered up his clothes, the sheer power of him even more vivid in the shaded outline.

"Are you going?" she asked softly. She wanted him to stay, wanted to feel his arms around her all night, but she could not yet allow him to know this. He had been right, she did feel as if she'd given in to a weakness and she was afraid to give him any further advantage over her. She had to think this all out, she told herself again. She needed to consider her entrance into the volatile world of emotional response.

"Yes," answered Buck curtly. Every tense line of his body showed his controlled anger. "I said we'd play by your rules, didn't I?" Then, suddenly, he swooped to bend over her, his arms on either side of her as he spoke harshly. "Can't you see we're meant for each other? Didn't tonight tell you anything?"

Confusion swept over her. She stared wordlessly up at him, at the gilt of his hair glinting in the dim light, at the shimmer of his dark eyes scanning her face, at the compressed line of the square lips almost hidden beneath the thick moustache. She was conscious of him as she had never been of any other man; her body needed his, but what kind of a foundation would that be for risking her commitment? On every other level, they were so different . . .

When she did not speak, Buck made a harsh, bitter sound that was a ghost of a laugh. "I'm wasting my damn time with you, aren't I? You're so wrapped up in your cocoon, you'll never let me have more than your body, will you? Well, hell, what am I complaining about—some men would kill to possess such loveliness!"

He made it sound like an insult and Searle flinched with the sting of it. But he stood and turned away, not seeing the pain in her eyes. His own disappointment lashed at him, frustrating him far more than his physical need for her had ever done. He'd felt triumphant tonight with her in his arms; her response had been as full, as vivid as his own and he'd thought he had reached her at last. But she'd made it clear that she wanted him only on the physical level and the knowledge stung him to the quick. He left, slamming doors all the way.

CHAPTER FOURTEEN

Searle let him go without protest. She had to confront her own emotions and she couldn't do that with him anywhere near her. Once he came within ten feet of her, she lost all ability to see things clearly, as if he were some powerful drug that dulled her mind. Perhaps he was a drug, addicting her body to his and clouding her understanding of herself. She wanted desperately to understand herself. Life before had always been clear—a portrait in black and white with no shadings to confuse the image. She knew what she wanted and why she wanted it. Now, she knew she wanted Buck Carlton, but she didn't know why and the question tormented her.

By midmorning, Searle no longer wished to think at all. Her head throbbed with the thoughts battling against one another in her mind. She wished her mind would go blank, take a day off and leave her in peace, but instead the assault continued, leaving her with a pounding headache, but no real answers.

Like a horse who refuses a jump time after time, whenever she came to the question of love, Searle refused to admit it. Backing away, she admitted her need, her jealousy, and her frustration over Buck Carlton, recognizing at last the deep involvement of her feelings as well as her physical desire. But the idea of love still frightened her—the New York experience and the miserable weeks that followed left her even more unwilling to chance being exposed to further hurt.

Buck had stripped away the veneer of her emotional shield and Searle resented him for it. Marbled thinly into her resentment was another, brighter emotion, but this she would not examine. Wandering about her apartment, listlessly waiting for something to happen, Searle retreated from deciphering precisely what she felt or why she felt it. The beauty of what she had experienced last night in Buck's arms seemed to exist on a different plane altogether from what she let herself think about him, about herself.

On a sudden impulse, she dragged a box from the back corner of her bedroom closet and rummaged through it until she found a framed photograph. She walked mechanically back to the living room, then stared at it with fixed concentration. Her parents on their wedding day. She had not known why she kept it, for it had been years since she had even glanced at it. Now, she studied it thoroughly and saw signs she'd never before noticed.

It had been her impression, left, she supposed, by her mother, that her parents had been madly in love when they first married, and that things had only gradually gone sour between them. Staring at the picture she held, Searle wondered. There was a bitter deepening at the corners of her mother's mouth that surely did not belong to the proverbial happy bride. There was a restless hint to her father's deep-set eyes. Perhaps there had never really been any love between them after all. And, then again, she thought with a heavy sigh, perhaps she was reading these things into the photo because she wanted to find them there.

But she and Buck would still be a mismatched pair. And, inevitably, that would lead to trouble. She always seemed to come back to the point she started from. She was beginning to realize that it wasn't what she felt for Buck that created the problem. It was what she would allow herself to risk feeling that mattered.

Just when the volcanic focus of her jumbled thoughts threatened to erupt, the harsh ring of her doorbell jarred her from her reflections, causing her to drop the photo. Ignoring the second imperative chime, she stared down at the broken glass, knowing this would be what she had been waiting for. She picked up the frame and laid it face down on her counter. The third ring was cut off as she opened the door.

"Good morning," said Buck tonelessly as he strolled into the room.

A grim cloud passed through his eyes as he took in her cool appearance; though she was casually dressed in a pair of white slacks and a flowered crepe blouse, she looked reserved, almost cautious. He felt a strong desire to slam his fist into something and it was with tight control that he spoke evenly.

"I came to settle a few things between us, Searle. I've agreed to play by your rules, but I'd like it understood that there will be no more games."

Without looking at him, Searle stooped to pick up the shards of glass from her floor. "Games?" she repeated.

"No more nights out with Norm—or any other guy. Not while you're seeing me. I won't share. Understood?"

His voice had lashed at her back. As she stood to face him, the bits of glass cupped in her palm, she felt all her worry, torment, and indecision crystallize into an emotion she clearly comprehended: pure anger. "No, it is not understood," she declared coldly. "If those are the rules, we might as well be married."

"Exactly," he agreed curtly.

She walked with deliberation into her kitchenette and dumped the broken glass into the trash. Then she came back out to perch on a barstool before responding as levelly as she could, "I told you, I'm not ready for that sort of commitment. You aren't going to force me into it simply to feed your macho ego."

"What ego?" inquired Buck tightly. "Whatever ego I had, you chewed up and spit out ages ago! I hardly think the remains of my ego have any bearing on our relationship."

"Ha! It has all the bearing on it," she returned tartly.

"It's been because your ego couldn't take a woman saying no to you that you've pursued me so hard. It's your ego that proposed to me, not you." She had meant the accusation to sound like a well-defined calculation; instead it sounded like a petulant grievance and, annoyed with herself, Searle shot a glance full of scornful censure at Buck.

She recognized the light beginning to appear in his eyes. He was looking, well, amused, and that further exacerbated her frayed temper. "Well?" she prodded. "Haven't you anything to say, Mr. Ego?"

"Oh, I've plenty to say to you, lady," he replied easily, too easily for Searle. "In my own good time."

"So, get on with it!" she snapped.

"First, we have to settle this matter of fidelity, Searle," he said calmly, but with an undertone of implacability. "On that, we have to go by my rule. No others—for either of us."

"I'm surprised you're prepared to sacrifice so much," remarked Searle. But the fire had gone out of her voice. Buck no longer looked or sounded angry and it was hard to stay inflamed when the other half of the argument refused to feed his share of kindling to the fire. She turned, leaning her elbows on the counter, and fiddled with the corner of the picture frame. "Did you get suspended?" she asked quietly.

Though she didn't look at him, Searle could almost feel his smile as he responded. He was clearly relaxed now. "No. I'll be hearing from the commissioner soon—and I'm certain the fine will be heavy—but Howe told me this morning there wouldn't be a suspension. Did you see the paper this morning?"

"No. I didn't want to see the sordid details."

"It wasn't too bad. Kraekor at least had the good sense not to tell the reporters who you were. There's a clear photo of him sprawled all over the floor, though," he said in a voice oozing with satisfaction.

Her head whipped around and she frowned at him. "You had no right to hit him! You can't go around hitting people just because they're with me."

His smile faded. "Just remember my rule and I won't be hitting anyone," he said tersely.

"So what if I don't agree to this rule of yours," said Searle, wanting to prick him, make him feel some of her own pain. "What then?"

The pause stretched out so long that Searle began to wish she hadn't said it. It sounded like a threat. Buck's face bore no hint of amusement now. He bore an unaccustomed blank expression, his eyes so distant that Searle feared he was going to turn and walk out. But at last, in a careful monotone, he answered her.

"Then I take a walk. It's one-on-one, Searle, or it's nothing. The choice is up to you."

Again her head bent over the counter, her loose hair spilling over her cheeks, hiding her face from him. She heard him breathe deeply, impatiently.

"Dammit, Searle!" he ground out. "What the hell has encased you in that don't-touch-me cocoon? Last night, I thought I could accept your body and forget the rest, but I realize now I've been choking up. I told you, I don't choke. I'm going to have it out of you if I have to kill to get it!"

As she whisked around to face him, her elbow cascaded into the photo frame, knocking it ajar. With a quick, guilty glance at Buck, she shoved it aside.

"What's that?" demanded Buck sharply.

"Just a picture," she said offhandedly.

He moved forward and reached before she could stop him. He turned it over and held it up, studying the couple in the photo. Judging by the fashions and hairstyles, it looked about thirty years old. "Who's this?" he queried, watching her closely with narrowed eyes.

"My parents." She said it as a prisoner of Auschwitz

might have said "Adolf Eichmann," with a cold, clear loathing that was far more expressive than a bitter invective.

He stared at the photo again. He saw the peculiar upward slant of the eyes in the woman, the sensuous full lower lip in the man, and he knew he held the key to Searle Delacorte. He wasn't quite sure where he would find the lock.

"Did they abuse you?" he probed carefully.

This was it, she realized. He was going to make her take that leap of the Grand Canyon whether she felt ready for it or not. In a voice void of emotion, she replied, "No, they didn't abuse me."

Stretching an arm out on either side of her, Buck braced himself against the countertop. Fixing his gaze on the dark lashes covering the secrets of her green eyes, he again pressed, "What did they do? Tell me, Searle."

"There's really nothing to tell," she said after a short pause. "They had a bad marriage, that's all. But it led me to decide that sort of relationship wasn't for me—ever."

"That's it?" he said, his tone incredulous. "Your folks had a bad marriage so you shut yourself off from life?"

"It wasn't a marriage so much as an emotional war. The main objective seemed to be wounding one another as often, as painfully as possible," she explained without inflection.

"And you were caught in the middle, left to bear the scars," said Buck gently.

"Oh, I was one of the major pieces of artillery," she said in a vain attempt at lightness. "I've always thought how fortunate it was for them they were given a ready-made spectator—the fight would surely have lost its spice without the audience."

Her bitterness drew him closer. Tilting her chin up with one tender hand, he forced her to look at him. "Listen,

Searle, we are not your parents. Whatever type of relationship they had, it's got nothing to do with us."

"You know what they say about familiarity," she said in a shaky voice of defense. "We'd soon be as contemptuous of one another as they were."

His fingers pressed into her skin. "You have to grow up and face life sometime, Searle. You have to quit running from your bad memories."

She felt trapped by him. She jerked her head free of his grasp and cried out desperately, "Can't you see? We aren't compatible! We've already begun the same pattern my parents fell into—we've argued so many times, I've lost count. And I even shouted at you—the first time in my life I ever raised my voice. It shocked me," she finished with a sorrow she could not hide.

Buck regarded her with a fixed intensity so harsh she felt the burn of it on her skin. "So rather than risk getting hurt, you continue to run away from life," he said flatly.

Unable to meet the searing darkness of his eyes, she bent her head and shrugged.

"Why?" He suddenly brought his hands up, roughly capturing the flesh of her arms, giving her a little shake. "What makes you think we couldn't turn our relationship into something quite different?"

"I've told you, but you won't listen," said Searle dully when he let her go. She had always known he wouldn't accept the truth, but felt no satisfaction in being proved right. She held up her long slender fingers and counted. "Item, we have nothing in common. Item, there's your habit of changing women like other men change shirts. Item—"

"Item," he broke in thickly, "there's this between us."

Catching her quickly, he drove his lips against hers, parting them, forcing her to admit her response. His hands came up to thread through her dark hair as he tilted her head back to deepen his kiss.

Searle was reaching up to take hold of him when he cast her away, stepping back. As her abrupt wave of desire receded, she noted with some surprise that he was shaking as he stood before her.

"What about that item, lady?" he demanded between short, sharp rasps.

She hesitated, wanting very much to take the leap he commanded of her, but hanging onto the edge, still afraid of the abyss of the unknown. Her hesitation flayed at Buck and he stepped farther away, shoving his hands into the pockets of his jeans as though he feared what he might do with them.

Scowling, he looked beyond her, catching sight of her wall clock and swearing. "I can't stay any longer or Howe *will* get me suspended! Are you coming to the game with me or not?"

His voice had a hostile ring to it that left Searle feeling unaccountably resentful. She shook her head, saw his eyes flare with anger, and bit out with an anger of her own, "You can't just expect me to fall into your arms because you say everything will be okay! I need to come to my own decisions. I have to think things through."

"So you still need to think about it?" he taunted harshly. "That's just great. You do that. Just don't deliberate too long, lady, or you may find the third strike whizzed past while you stood waiting at the plate." He whirled and slammed forcefully out, shaking the walls of her apartment as he did so.

His angry departure left her feeling emptier than ever. She knew she had said and done all the wrong things, but hadn't seemed able to stop herself. She set the portrait of her parents upright and glared at it. "Damn you," she whispered. "Damn you both."

Searle had always believed that she existed in her emotional vacuum by choice. Now she realized it had been thrust upon her by the instability of her parents. The anguished lessons they'd taught her on how to give and to receive love had warped her from an early age, and until Searle saw beyond those lessons, she had really had no choice at all.

But Buck Carlton had stormed into her life, offering her a choice at last. Searle simply did not know if she was ready to take it. Her life had always been so independent, so well-ordered. She had been completely satisfied. Then Buck had given her isolated existence a mighty shake, sifting out emotions she had not known she possessed and leaving her filled with doubts and questions she feared to answer.

After a while, Searle collected the photograph and rounded the corner of her kitchenette. There, she calmly threw the picture on top of the broken shards of glass in the trash can beneath her sink. Buck was right. Bad memories should be thrown away, forgotten. She should have tossed hers out years ago, instead of leaving them to eat away at her chance for happiness.

Having taken some small action, she felt immeasurably better. She still wasn't certain what it was she wanted, but she knew she wanted to find out. That was a massive start. Her headache disappeared with her sour outlook and, gathering up her purse, Searle left the swirl of her thoughts behind in her apartment as she went for a drive.

Somehow, she found herself ending up at Stillwater Lake. She parked her car, then wandered down through reedy grasses to sit with her toes dipping in the water's edge. Buck would like doing this, she thought, then blushed as fiercely as if she'd imagined something quite other than this innocent pastime. It was true, they did have a lot in common. Even if they had had nothing at all, Searle doubted she could have disliked him for long. She did like him. He was intelligent, charming, understanding. She was a fool!

A new contentment swept over as she laughed out loud.

Love, commitment—these things were still the big question marks. But whatever rules they played by, Searle knew she wanted to be in the game. If she was honest with herself, she had truly known since last night that she could no longer contemplate being without Buck.

Jumping up, she drove back to her apartment. She prepared to confront Buck by immersing herself in a long, relaxing bath, then dressing with infinite care. As evening wore into night, Searle's newfound elation dulled to frustrated anger, then to a numb sadness. By midnight, she realized he wasn't coming, he wasn't calling. *Here,* she scolded herself bitterly, *is what happens whenever one takes a chance on emotional happiness.* She reasoned that Buck was deliberately making her suffer for the things she'd said earlier and scoffed at his claim of loving her. She reminded herself coldly that she would have to remember that loving is a twin to hating.

Reconstructing her wall of indifference was a painful process, but by the next morning, Searle was vowing not to let herself be hurt by Buck anymore. She felt as though he had taken advantage of her and swung between never wanting to see him again and dying to tell him to his face what she thought of him.

Shortly before noon, on her way to the company cafeteria, Searle caught sight of Norm Kraekor standing by his desk. He didn't hear her come up behind him, and jumped nervously when she laid her hand on his sleeve. He turned sharply around and Searle gasped at the sight of his black-and-blue eye, swollen nearly shut.

"Oh, Norm, I'm so sorry—" she began.

He threw a rapid glance over her shoulder, then his. "Why didn't you tell me you had something going with Carlton?" he demanded petulantly. "I'd never have taken you there if I'd known!"

"But we . . ." Her voice trailed away. She couldn't deny

that something had gone on. "Are you very badly hurt?" she asked instead.

"Humph!" snorted Norm. He'd promised himself never to get within a hundred yards of Searle Delacorte again; he began backing away from her as if her presence constituted a threat to his health.

"I am sorry, Norm," said Searle earnestly. "I never meant for you to get hurt."

"Ah, it's okay," he muttered, not sounding mollified. Then he perked up a bit. "At least I didn't go into the hospital. Served him right!" he added mysteriously.

"Served who?"she asked absently. She had apologized to Norm, now she was anxious to get on with her lunch.

"Carlton, of course," answered Norm with a smile that pronounced his belief that there was, after all, justice in the world.

He had her attention now. "Buck?" she queried stupidly. "Buck Carlton?"

"Hey, didn't you know?" returned Norm. He watched with concern as the color fled from Searle's face.

"Know what? Are you saying Buck is in the hospital?" she asked, a frantic note clear in her voice. She put one hand out to brace herself against his desk.

"Look, doll, don't worry," said Norm quickly. "He got hurt in yesterday's game, sliding hard into third base. Last I heard, they thought he might have broken his ankle or something and they carted him off to the hospital."

"Broken ankle?" She felt ridiculously dull. She couldn't seem to understand what Norman was telling her.

"Yeah." He squinted at her with his good eye. "How come you didn't know?"

"I—I really couldn't face the sports news . . . Do you know what hospital he's in?" she asked sharply, straightening.

"St. Luke's, I think. You okay, now?"

The color crept back into her cheeks. She nodded briskly, then pushed past him without another word. He stood shaking his head, wondering why he'd ever gotten mixed up with such a crazy dame. Searle didn't remember to move her marker as she passed Millie's desk on her way out. She was too busy trying to think how she would greet him, how she would react if he was cold to her. As she drove along the freeway, she asked herself again and again, why hadn't he called to let her know? Why hadn't he let her know?

CHAPTER FIFTEEN

The woman at the information desk eyed Searle with all the warmth of a polar icecap.

"Visitation is restricted," she repeated in the nasal monotone that convinced Searle she was a computer.

The proffered press card earned Searle nothing more than a withering glance of piteous scorn, so she whirled in disgust and exited. Five minutes later, she reentered by another door and slipped past the desk into the elevator bank looking precisely as if she knew where she was going. She didn't, but she was certain she wasn't leaving the hospital without attempting to find Buck.

Every floor looked depressingly the same to her. People passed through long, impersonal linoleum corridors with a sense of purpose, ignoring the myriad of medicinal smells and hushed metallic clatter that surrounded them. Searle wandered each floor, peeking into rooms and trying to appear as unobtrusive as possible. Every time someone in hospital white or green passed by, she tensed, poised to dart away at the first challenge, but no one even bothered to look at her. She was nothing more than another in an ever-changing sea of faces. She began to be thankful that she had never been ill enough to have been hospitalized.

Rounding a corner on the third floor, she found herself unexpectedly faced with a brightly painted yellow-and-green wall. A small sign beside the open double doors announced PEDIATRICS. She turned to retrace her steps when she heard a low, rumbling laugh that froze her into place.

Glancing over her shoulder to make certain she wasn't seen, Searle stepped through the double doors and followed the direction of that laugh. To her right was a short hall that opened onto a wide area filled with small tables and chairs, shelves and boxes, all brightly painted. Several children were camped around a man seated in a wheelchair, their shrill childish laughter harmonizing with the man's deep tones.

Searle stepped to the side of the door frame, remaining out of sight as she watched Buck captivate the children with a story, illustrating it with broad sweeps of his long arms. She could not hear his words, only the cheerful tone of his voice, but she saw the small, upturned faces fixed steadfastly on his and knew his audience was enraptured. Some of the children were smiling out of faces that had known too much pain to look young and Searle felt her heart wrench.

Suddenly, the golden head tipped back as another laugh filled the room, the wheelchair rolling slightly with the motion. It was as if the kaleidescope had shifted and suddenly all the little bits of glass had fallen into a clear shape. Searle moved quickly away before he could turn and see her, then left the way she had come.

Seeing Buck there, the sunlight brilliantly gilding his hair as he bestowed precious moments of happiness on those children, Searle had at last seen herself clearly. At last she knew without doubt that she loved Buck Carlton. More, she knew she wanted to love him. It was a moment so striking that she had to get away, be alone, sort it all out and comprehend the wonder of it.

She drove to a nearby park and leisurely strolled along a narrow dirt path, letting her eyes roll over the dazzle of the sun-dappled water of the pond, over the light and shadow twined around every tree. Years of emotional withdrawal had not been easily overcome. The instinct to retreat from her feelings had been too deeply ingrained for Searle not to fight the process of shedding her isolation. But the armor had dropped away from her in the hospital, totally and irrevocably. Even if Buck no longer wanted her, Searle knew she would suffer the pain and go on, but she would never again hide behind a shield of benumbed indifference. It would mean risking getting hurt terribly, but it also meant enjoying, for the first time in her life, all the happiness life could offer. Her years as an emotional cripple were over.

After wandering for a time, Searle left the path and dropped to the grass, where she sat in the warmth of the sunlight, idly pulling up bits of green and letting them drop carelessly from her hand. Would he still want her? she wondered. And how would she communicate to him that she would give him everything—including commitment? He had not called her last night and that scared her, but if she had to go to him on her knees, Searle knew she would make every effort to convince him to give her another chance.

She finally recognized that the feeling mixed with her resentment toward Buck had been relief. Relief that she would no longer have to live hidden behind a shield, isolated from others. She had never admitted to loneliness before, always believing she had made the choice to live alone and was, therefore, not lonely. But she had been secretly craving affection for years. It had taken Buck Carlton to make her realize that.

Letting herself fall gently back, Searle lay content. Her nostrils filled with the vivid, clean scent of earth and grass and her skin warmed with the caress of the sun. Despite the pain it could cause, love was the enrichment of life. She knew this now. Whatever her parents had felt, it had been too twisted to be love. Love made you responsible for someone's happiness; it made someone indispensable to yours. She remembered all the little joys of being with Buck and all the long, empty hours without him and knew that, for her, love meant Buck.

When the sun began to tilt downward, Searle was surprised. She'd felt such contentment, been so at peace with herself, that she had not noticed the day fading away. Stretching languidly, she rose and brushed the clinging grass from the skirt of her jade-green dress. As she readjusted the positioning of the thin belt at her waist, she thought out what she would tell Lenn to explain her absence for the afternoon. Then she pulled the pins from her hair, dropping them onto the ground, and shook her hair loose before sauntering back to her car.

She arrived back at her apartment in time to catch the local evening news, so she carried her portable TV set into the living room and tuned in. She was hoping they would give word on Buck's injury and was highly annoyed when the peal of her doorbell cut through the air just as the sportscaster came on. Realizing it had to be Norman stopping by, wishing him a million miles away, she threw open the door with a cross frown set on her face.

The yellow wood of a crutch pushed over her threshold, followed by another, and Buck Carlton hopped back into her life. He saw her frown as he crossed into the living room and instantly matched it with one of his own. Before she had a chance to speak, he whirled on his crutches and ground out, "Look, lady, I've about had it with you! I've proposed and I've pleaded—I've tried about every damn play on the field! But when I started to play sloppy ball because I couldn't get you out of my mind, I knew that was it!"

Her heart was leaping so joyously, Searle was surprised he couldn't hear it. How could he not see the love glowing in her eyes? she wondered, but she merely put in, "It was?"

"It was," he said grimly. "I thought because I loved you like crazy I'd be willing to settle for whatever crumbs you let me have, but I'm not."

"You're not?" She loved hearing the rasp of his voice, seeing him lean, weighted on one foot, and lecture to her. She loved everything about him. His thick untidy hair, which was gilded on top but darkly threaded on the ends; his sandy moustache, which always tilted with expression as he spoke; his deep sable eyes that so often twinkled with laughter—just everything. Even his faded blue jeans, which clung sensuously low on his hips. She loved him and she hoped he would go on telling her of his love forever, so she stood meekly, looking blank.

"Hell, no," returned Buck in the sort of voice an attorney used to sway the jury. "I'm not a halfway man and I detest getting stranded on base. Now, Searle Delacorte, either you take a chance on me or you don't. It's that simple."

"It is?"

"It is. You can't go on hiding from life, Searle. You think you've got a nice, safe, comfortable sort of life, but all you've got is nothing. You're losing the game, lady, and you'll never score one if you don't take a chance. You don't score, you don't win, that's it."

"And if I take a chance?" she asked, wondering how she kept the delirium of happiness she felt out of her voice.

"You may get hurt, but not from me, Searle, I promise you that." Buck grimaced, sending his moustache up crookedly and her heart into another bounding of joy. "Maybe you're right and we are a mismatched pair. But I don't give a damn whether you like beer or rock and roll or even baseball. I just want you to try liking *me*. We'll never know if we could work it out unless we give it a try."

"You're right," said Searle softly.

"And so, maybe you're right and some people use each other." He brandished his crutch, pointing it to emphasize his argument. "But however different our tastes, I don't think we're like that. I don't think we'd deliberately set out to hurt one another."

"Neither do I," she agreed on a whisper.

"So this is it—you risk getting on the scoreboard or

I—" He stopped, brows lowering. "What did you say?" he demanded.

"I said, neither do I," she answered with an outward thrust of her lower lip.

"And before that," he prodded, "what did you say before that?"

"I said, you're right," she replied. The thrust slid up into a smile and for a moment Buck stopped breathing altogether. "I think we should try to work it out. I want to try, Buck, really I do."

"Well, hell's bells," he said with a deep breath. He stared at her so fixedly that Searle felt the color suffuse her cheeks with a heated glow. The angry flash of his eyes altered, becoming a flame so dark the brown became a deep black.

"Come here," he ordered suddenly, his voice thickened.

Searle came. He let his crutches drop, then fell against her, knocking her off balance. They toppled to the floor together, laughing breathlessly. As he folded his body over hers, the weight of him on top of her had a naturalness to it that Searle recognized. This was where, she decided, he was meant to be. His lips were caressing her temple, his breath stirring her hair, and her body went limp with total submission. Buck felt it and with a stifled gasp, he enslaved her mouth with his own.

Because this time she held nothing back, the kiss had a heady depth that affected them both like a potent drug. When Buck reluctantly drew away, they were both gasping for air.

She ran her eyes possessively over the supple length of him, then halted at the swathes tightly wrapped around his left foot. "What—what's wrong with your foot?" she asked in a voice suddenly deep with concern.

"Pulled some tendons sliding into third yesterday," he answered, muffling his words against the arc of her throat.

"Why—why didn't you call to let me know?" inquired

Searle, half wanting an answer and half wanting him to go on kissing her.

He withdrew from her at that and propped himself on his elbow. Gazing at her as if he could not believe she were real, he let his hand play along the soft curves of her figure for a long moment before replying. "I thought you must know, that you'd have heard about it," he said at last, an anger at the memory tingling his tone. "I thought it proved you didn't care when you weren't trying to get a hold of me. That really hurt, and a hell of a lot more than my ankle."

"I didn't know until this afternoon. When you didn't come or call last night, I was sure it meant you'd decided not to wait for me to make up my mind and I"—she lowered her lashes to hide the renewal of the pain she'd felt then—"I didn't know if I could go on with the motions of living without you."

She felt the heat of his breath as his lips caressed each of her closed lids. Then her eyes flew open to drown in the tide of love engulfing her from the depths of his gaze.

"Say it, Searle," he whispered, his voice ragged. "Please say it."

She understood. Without hesitation, she said clearly, "I love you, Buck. I love you."

He groaned and she was amazed to realize he was trembling as his arms went around her once more. They clung to one another as if clinging to the last moment of life and for several long moments neither was capable of conscious thought. Then a shudder rippled through Buck and he rasped quietly into her ear, "When did you know? This morning? Last night?"

She shivered with pleasure at the feel of his lips on her earlobe, then answered breathlessly, "Well, you rather sneaked up on me. Before I began to realize the danger of getting involved with you, I *was* involved."

He drew back abruptly, staring at her in stunned accusation. "You knew that long ago? You knew and you let us go on—"

"No, I always refused to see it," she cut in quickly, "especially after you proposed. That really shook me. I'd lived through a marriage of misfits and I wasn't about to do so again." She quavered with a deep draw of air. "I know now I was so frightened because deep down I wanted to say yes. I wanted to try, Buck, but I was too afraid of getting hurt, of failing. I told you, I don't like to make a bad job of anything."

He stroked her cheek gently, then lightly skimmed his lips along the path of his hands. "Neither do I, my love, neither do I. I knew something was wrong—I couldn't accept that you would turn me off for no reason—"

"Egotist!" she chided lightly.

"But I was certain it had to have been a man who messed you up and I was sick with jealousy. Half the time I wanted to punch somebody out—"

"You were doing pretty well at it," she put in dryly.

"And the other half I wanted to pull you into bed with me," he finished with a series of tiny, teasing kisses across the neckline of her dress. Her breast rose quickly with excitement and his hand palmed it, his fingers delicately splaying over the dress's thin material. "So when, my sweet, darling love, did you finally know you loved me?"

She ran her palm along the rough plane of his cheek, considering. "I think I really knew I loved you back in New York—"

"You what?" he interrupted in disbelief.

"The minute you walked out on me in the hotel, I knew I loved you," she admitted, her voice saddened. "But it was so painful—just as I'd always thought love would be—that I forced myself to overcome it. I told myself you'd only hurt me more if you knew you had me in your power and I told myself it was for the best. But I hurt all the time."

"So did I, you little fool," said Buck roughly. He turned his head and kissed her hand before she could withdraw it. "I'd thought I'd lost you. I spent every night aching for you. I'm not used to rejection and when you shut me out that night . . . I knew I'd rushed you, but it still hurt like hell. Knowing you didn't feel the way I did gnawed at me constantly. I needed you—"

"Past tense?" she broke in, lightly teasing him.

"And present and future," he replied with a kiss on each of her high cheekbones. "So when I saw you with that jerk Saturday night, all my resolutions to forget you just vanished. I had to have you, Searle, like an addict needs his fix."

"I need you, too, I see that now," she murmured.

"When did you admit you loved me?" he asked again, breathing unsteadily as her fingers roamed lithely over his neck and chest.

"Today. I went up to the hospital—"

"I didn't see you!" he exclaimed.

"I know. I couldn't get your room number from the robot at the front desk, so I slipped past her and wandered around looking for you. Unpleasant places, hospitals," she added under her breath. "Then I heard you laugh and watched you in the children's ward, with all the kids hanging on your every word—"

"So you're the one," he half whistled.

"The one what?"

"A couple of kids said they saw a beautiful lady watching us, but when I wheeled the chair around, no one was there. To think I just missed you," he finished shakily.

Her fingers were slowly undoing the buttons of his shirt and Searle could feel the erratic thudding of his heart. The tremulous rhythm thrilled her. She kept her eyes fixed on the buttons, unable to chance looking up.

"I knew when I saw you today that I loved you, Buck. But even more, I knew that I wanted to love you, whether

I got hurt or not. I was afraid you'd reject me now and I went to the park and wandered around, thinking up methods to convince you to give me another chance."

"And all day I tried to reach you here and at your office and when I couldn't get through I demanded that they let me out of that damn hospital or I was going to break every damn door getting out," he said with a rueful smile. "I didn't know quite what I was going to do if you told me to go ahead and walk out . . ."

Searle kissed away the pain she saw flicker briefly in his sable eyes. The sound of a commercial blared out, capturing their attention. Buck shifted his weight to cast a quizzical glance at the set resting on the countertop.

"What's that?"

"A television," she answered promptly.

He punished her with a teasing nibble on her earlobe until she breathlessly confessed, "I got it a few weeks ago so I could watch all your games. And the ones I couldn't watch, I listened to on the radio."

The flare of desire ignited within his eyes, inflaming her own need. Buck moved, his thighs rubbing restlessly against hers, and Searle felt the coarse bandages at his ankle chaff her leg. She looked at him with renewed concern.

"Your pulled tendons—is it a very serious injury?"

"Nah. I'll have to stay off it awhile, but I'll begin working with the trainer tomorrow and it won't be long before I'm back in uniform," he explained. "I wouldn't mind missing this next road trip, though," he added as a husky afterthought.

"But what about your hitting record?" she asked, ignoring the invitation in his gaze.

"There's always next season. Hell, I've lost my privacy, my free time—and besides you're the only thing I've given a damn about since July."

"Oh?" responded Searle with an arched brow. "Then

just why have you been doing so well? I should think not having me would have put you off your game."

"Worried, were you?" he bantered, his voice low and loving. "You were the reason, Searle. The mere thought of you kept my adrenaline pumping steadily. Like now," he explained with another deep kiss that took her senses on a roller-coaster ride.

"You said you were persistent," remarked Searle on a throaty laugh as he reluctantly released her lips. "But I was surprised when you kept coming back. Any other guy would have given me up as a hopeless case long ago."

"I nearly did once or twice," he confessed. He pressed his mouth into her hair, just above her ear, and she quivered as his warm breath grazed her cheek. "But I knew you weren't frigid. I'd seen flashes of the fire in those emerald eyes of yours right from the first and I wanted to get the woman promised in those flashes."

"Umm," she mumbled, her lips following the mold of his neck. "When did you decide you loved me?"

"I'm not sure. I wanted you right on sight. But you were so damn untouchable! The first night you went out with Norman—"

"I didn't—"

"But I thought you had—"

Their breaths mingled together in a lengthy pause. With a feathery touch, Buck sketched the line of her lips with one fingertip. "That night, I kept picturing you with him. I'd never been jealous before and it was eating at me. I went through hell just thinking about you being with him. When I came by the next day, I only meant to find out what, if anything, you'd done with him. The next thing I knew I was blurting out a proposal and then wishing I'd cut my tongue out."

"Because you asked me to marry you?"

"Because I thought I'd scared you off. By then, I knew I wanted to marry you come hell or high water. I still do."

Her hands were under the fabric of his shirt, massaging the muscles of his chest and back with a deliberately sensual touch. He pressed closer to her, trapping her beneath his body, and she felt the desire throbbing within him.

"When?" he murmured thickly.

"Now, if you like," she replied on a wicked whisper of delight.

"When will you marry me?" he expanded as his tongue flicked the corner of her mouth.

"Now, if you like," she repeated, her voice thick with emotion.

His lips claimed hers, letting her know just how much he would like it.

LOOK FOR NEXT MONTH'S CANDLELIGHT ECSTASY ROMANCES™

98 AS NIGHT FOLLOWS DAY, *Suzanne Simmons*
99 GAMBLER'S LOVE, *Amii Lorin*
100 NO EASY WAY OUT, *Elaine Raco Chase*
101 AMBER ENCHANTMENT, *Bonnie Drake*
102 SWEET PERSUASION, *Ginger Chambers*
103 UNWILLING ENCHANTRESS, *Lydia Gregory*
104 SPEAK SOFTLY TO MY SOUL, *Dorothy Ann Bernard*
105 A TOUCH OF HEAVEN, *Tess Holloway*